I0583151

AFTER EVENING

A NOVEL

STUART FABE

After Evening

Copyright 2018 by Stuart A. Fabe

All Rights Reserved

No part of this publication may be reproduced, stored in a retrieval system, or transmitted, in any form or by any means—electronic, mechanical, photo-reproductive, recording, or otherwise—without prior written permission by the publisher, except for the inclusion of brief quotations in a review.

For more information about this title or to order other books and/or electronic media, contact the publisher:

Stuart A. Fabe
Greencastle, Indiana
stuartfabe@gmail.com

ISBN: 978-0-692-93582-8

Printed in the United States

Author's Note

Plots are the vehicles on which stories ride. Characters are their pilots and passengers.

After Evening is a work of fiction and is written solely for entertainment. This story is a sequel to my second novel, *Evening Comes,* and readers will recognize some familiar characters. I hope you enjoy!

Dedication

In loving memory of my parents,
Robert and Miriam Fabe,
and to Alan and Donna Stanley
with eternal affection and gratitude.

Chapter 1

Everyone has secrets.
Everyone has said, done, or witnessed
things they prefer not to talk about.
I'm no different.
My secrets, if known beyond my
small circle of friends,
could unravel a life that in many ways is ideal . . .
my own.

CAN'T REMEMBER THE LAST TIME I slept soundly through the night. I don't suffer from disturbing dreams or urges to use the bathroom. I just wake up and see faces. This shouldn't be too disturbing because, as a photographer, I've shot a lot of portraits

throughout my career. It's just that some faces bring a smile to my face, while others, well let's just say, not so much.

My name is Clay Arnold. I'm a freelance photographer of some renown which means I make a very good living traveling the world on photographic assignments that I find personally appealing. My home is in a renovated nineteenth-century beer brewery situated along the White River north of Indianapolis, Indiana. It's also where I have my photographic darkroom and my antique camera museum that is open to the public. Most importantly, it's where my close family of friends also resides. Oh, and there's one other thing . . . I'm an avenging vigilante.

So what does that mean exactly? That I'm an avenging vigilante. Yes, it's true that I've executed several domestic terrorists and right-wing racist jerks who I felt deserved it. Yes, if I were totally honest, I would agree that I've felt a bit self-righteous about terminating bad guys . . . the whole judge, jury, and executioner thing wrapped up in one neat, stealthy package. And again honestly, I'm generally comfortable with being a vigilante, but I have to admit that secrecy about this comes at a price. And it's my NOT being forthright with some people, meaning the woman I love, Maggie Bodine, that I feel an ever-growing need to come totally clean with her. I'm just not sure how, without losing her.

Right now as I contemplate these issues I'm sitting on the roof-garden balcony just off my bedroom in the old brewery that I own. It's past midnight on this moonless late summer night, and I can easily see a vast stellar arm of the Milky Way as it stretches across the southern sky. The soft celestial light illuminates the old brewery complex which includes my home and camera museum, plus the original farmhouse where my life-long friends Tori and Weed Rawlins live, and the old power plant where Mace, Rennie, and Lex live. And, in the center of these structures is the cobblestone courtyard built by the Block brothers when they emigrated from Bavaria and opened their beer brewery in 1855. It's our home.

I turn down the music on my sound system and take a slow draw on my glass of Four Roses bourbon. The soft burn glides down my throat and settles into my senses. I inhale the intoxicating vapors, close my eyes, and listen to the night. A lingering chill comes over me as I flash back on the terrifying events that threatened so many lives over the last two years: my beautiful fiancé's murder, the Hacker men's assault on the hospital and insurance company in Indianapolis, and the final violent conflict here within the familial confines of our old brewery complex. And of course, there were my personal executions while on photographic assignments in

Charleston, Santa Fe, San Diego, Palm Springs, and Chicago . . . all cities that I love and now all cities with a stain. Another chill hits me to my core, and I stare heavenward for some relief.

And relief comes as I am suddenly joined by my trusted friend, Satchmo, who is the largest darn Maine Coon cat that you ever saw. I've often thought that Satchmo is like a silver-gray ghost appearing and dematerializing in the blink of an eye. He is also a major confidante of some things that shall remain our little secrets. A moment later Satchmo sways in my direction and rubs his furry flank against my lower legs. He exhales an audible snuffle and drops a lifeless rodent by my feet. In an instant he is gone to complete his appointed rounds, and I am alone again with my thoughts, a dead rodent, and the beating of my heart.

Minutes pass in relative silence. The night sky has become my friend. On any clear night I try to spend at least a few minutes looking in all directions, testing my memory about the constellations and their alpha stars. Tonight the stars look like diamonds cast onto a great black velvet cloth. They are totally mesmerizing and their vastness presents an impossible challenge for me to try to comprehend. I close my eyes and take another draw on my glass of bourbon. Again I deeply inhale the liquor's vapors and let them have their way with my senses. I open my eyes to see the constellation Perseus as he swoops down to save Andromeda from the dreaded sea monster, Cetus. An act of classical heroism that has repeated itself each night for eons.

In recent months, especially when I couldn't be with Maggie, I've turned my camera to the night sky to capture the glorious multitude above. It has filled a void in my life, and I feel that I have taken some of my very finest images ever. At least that's what the art critics and gallery owners seem to say.

From the courtyard below, I hear the faint tremolo of a blues harmonica, and I know my lifelong friend, Maurice "Weed" Rawlins, is out and about, probably on the front porch of the brewery farmhouse where he and his sister, Tori, live.

"Hey Weed, is that you?" I call down to him.

"Yeah, I was thinking you might still be awake," Weed replied. "Do you want a little company? I have something for you."

"Sure thing, come on up." I encouraged.

Twenty seconds later I could hear the whir of my home elevator and Weed materializes on my deck.

"What's up?" Weed began.

"Actually, Perseus, Cassiopeia, Andromeda, and a few gazillion other starry sights, but that's probably not what you're asking."

"Right," Weed confirmed. "I thought you might enjoy this newspaper clipping about your recent award."

"Oh that, sure. Thanks, Weed. That was a very complimentary award from some pretty heady folks involved in astrophotography. I'm really glad Maggie was able to join me for the awards ceremony. Exciting night!"

"Very complimentary award?!" Weed repeated. "You get the 'Astrophotographer of the Year' award from the most prestigious astronomy magazine on the planet, and the best you can say is 'very complimentary'!?"

But Weed knew better. "Tori and I have known you virtually all of our lives, and we still marvel at your modesty for a photographic career that has received accolade upon accolade ever since we were in high school."

"Yeah, it's been a great ride," I agreed, "and my recent fascination with photographing the night sky has opened up new worlds for me, pardon the pun."

Weed handed me the newspaper clipping that showed me at a recent awards reception, holding the winner's gold medallion, with Maggie Bodine beaming at my side.

"Yeah, that was quite an awards ceremony," I acknowledged. "Especially considering the talented competition I was up against. Seriously, I felt honored just to be considered in their league."

I continued, "I guess I haven't had a chance to tell you about something else that's pretty humbling, too. The President of Kissinger College in Greencastle called me yesterday and said they want me to come to the college next month and receive an honorary doctorate. I'm still stunned and actually pretty excited about it. I'd love it if we could all go as a family. It would mean a lot to me."

"Well, smell you!" Weed chortled. "That's amazing! Congratulations! You never cease to amaze us. Of course, we'll all be there!"

Weed and I sat down by the patio table, and I offered my lifelong pal a glass of Four Roses bourbon which he amicably accepted. The two of us sat quietly for a few minutes taking in the night's sounds.

Then Weed sincerely asked, "Do you think much about what we all went through the last couple of years?"

I sighed and said, "Yeah, enough, I suppose. I never would've guessed that we would be exposed to so much death and destruction as we were. I suppose what I think about most is losing Jennifer to that bombing of her Planned Parenthood Center and how close we came to losing Tori, Mace, Rennie, and Lex . . . and you, Weed." I shivered at the thought.

"But, we survived it," Weed consoled. "We stick together."

"Yeah, we do," I firmly agreed. "We all stick together, and what a colorful lot we are. It's like Mace said during our Thanksgiving dinner last year: 'Look at us! What a hodgepodge of humanity. We've got us a ghetto kid, a blind woman, an old black man, a guy who goes by the name "Weed", and a self-appointed vigilante. On top of that we have a three-legged dog, and a huge cat that thinks he's human. And, I wouldn't have it any other way.'"

Both men nodded their agreement with their friend, Mace Davis's, sage words.

A moment later Satchmo reappeared and jumped up on the table close to Weed and me. He proudly laid another lifeless rodent on the table for his two humans to admire and bounded off to continue his nighttime wanderings.

"What say we see if Mace wants to join us for breakfast tomorrow at Stella's Diner," Weed suggested. "I think Tori and Rennie are going to work in the vegetable garden and maybe do some school work."

"Sounds like a good plan," I agreed. "We haven't seen Stella for a couple of weeks, and I miss her perspicacious personality. You want to text Mace? Maybe we can meet in the courtyard around eight o'clock."

"Oh, I think Mace'll be delighted to see Stella. You gotta love a savvy businesswoman who wears hot-pink fluffy tops with skintight pants!" Weed deadpanned. "I'll see you tomorrow."

After Weed left, I sat outside for a few minutes longer and looked at my watch. Twelve forty-five a.m. It really wasn't too late to call Maggie since she lives in Santa Fe, but I didn't want to begin a serious telephone conversation when what I need to say to her should be done in person. I know I need to talk with her very soon, though. I love her very much, and my secrets carry a heavy burden.

Chapter 2

WALLACE BANE SHUFFLED around in his dimly lit office in the basement of the Von Timm Observatory in Greencastle, Indiana. His twenty-five-year career as assistant-to-the-chief-astronomer at Kissinger College was as poorly illuminated by anything scholarly as was his subterranean office space. Simply stated, Wallace Bane's astronomy career never got off the ground because he never acquired the academic credentials like his university colleagues did, and he never published anything noteworthy, until recently. As much as anything though, most people were just repelled by his unattractive appearance and his pathetic insecurities. In

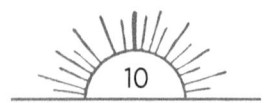

short, Wallace Bane was an academic underachiever who people just didn't like to be around.

Despite these professional and personal shortcomings, Wallace Bane was devoted to the night sky. On the rare occasions when the telescope was not in use by his superiors, he enjoyed attaching his camera onto the observatory's 1885 Clark telescope and taking astronomical images. Unfortunately, like most of his professional attempts, many of his images were nice enough but nothing great when compared with images taken by other serious astrophotographers, including the lowest of the lows . . . damn amateurs!

Wallace "The Mole" Bane, as his colleagues called him because he labored underground, muttered to himself as he sifted through the stack of papers on his cluttered desk.

"Ah, there you are!" Wallace said to himself as he found the letter of commendation from *Space and Beyond* magazine which he recently received. Wallace had entered three images into the annual Night Sky Contest and had been recognized along with eight other commendation recipients. Despite being only one of nine recipients, he beamed with pride at his commendation. However, his pride was short-lived when he realized that three others had also won the silver and bronze medals, and of course, the prestigious Astrophotographer of the Year gold medallion.

The Mole cringed when he scanned the names of the other winners, and he let out a baleful moan when he saw Clay Arnold's name as the top winner.

"Damn amateur!" he bellowed. "I don't care that Clay Arnold is a famous photographer. He's a rookie to astrophotography, and I've been taking night pictures for twenty years. Mine dammit! This award should've been mine!"

Wallace the Mole shuffled through more papers on his desk and grabbed on to the newspaper article and photograph showing Clay Arnold with the winner's gold medallion. Wallace's eyes then fell on the image of the beautiful woman standing next to Clay Arnold. The caption read Maggie Bodine.

"Tarnation, that newbie jerk, Clay Arnold, even has a pretty girlfriend!"

For the next five minutes, Wallace the Mole staggered around his subterranean office, sneering and shouting creative obscenities as he looked at his puny letter of commendation next to the picture of Clay Arnold with his gold medal and the lovely Maggie Bodine. "Aaaarrrgghhh!"

Wallace heard a sharp knock on his office door followed by a loud voice that shouted, "Are you okay in there, Mr. Bane?" It was not lost on anyone that all of Wallace's colleagues had earned PhDs and were called doctor, and he alone was referred to as "mister". It was the department chairman and chief astronomer, Dr. Mortimer Chestnut. Wallace tried to compose himself, but Dr. Chestnut knocked loudly again and then forced the office door open.

"What's going on in here?" Dr. Chestnut demanded as he looked around Mister Bane's disheveled office. He thought it looked more like a jail cell with its stone walls and bare lightbulbs. In fact, it originally was a caretaker's quarters with a small commode and sink in the corner and a locked storage area beyond. He stared at Wallace and again asked, "What's going on? I heard loud shouts and curses and thought surely you must be in agony or something."

Wallace stared back at his chief astronomer, and made up an excuse. "Oh, I accidentally slammed my finger in the desk drawer, sir," he lied. "Sorry about the noise. I didn't think anyone would hear me down here in the bowels of the observatory . . . sir."

"Yes, well, quite right," Dr. Chestnut said. "It is pretty soundproof down here, isn't it, Mr. Bane?"

"Yes, sir," came Wallace's pitiful reply. "Is there something I may do for you, sir?"

It had been months since Dr. Chestnut had last ventured into Wallace Bane's subterranean realm. He continued to gaze around at the dungeon-like space that Wallace inhabited, and he cringed at the thought of existing in such a dreary space.

A moment later Dr. Chestnut looked back at his subordinate and recalled his original reason for seeking Wallace out. "Uh, yes, there is something you can do for me, Mr. Bane. As you may know, the board of trustees for Kissinger College will be holding their annual meeting early next month when school resumes. As part of the ceremonies, President Murray and I have encouraged the board to confer an honorary doctorate on our fellow Hoosier, Clay Arnold, for his recent selection as Astrophotographer of the Year. The board unanimously has agreed to this, and Mr. Arnold has graciously accepted our invitation."

"Lovely," Wallace Bane managed to say. "What may I do to help, sir?"

"Well, I'm sure Clay Arnold's visit to Kissinger College will no doubt include a visit to our modest, but beloved Von Timm Observatory. I need you to make certain that the entire facility, both inside and out, is spotless and that the Clark telescope is in tip-top shape for any celestial viewing we may be asked to provide. Is that understood, Mr. Bane? Tip-top!"

"Yes, sir! Tip-top, Dr. Chestnut!" came Wallace the Mole's subservient reply.

"Oh, and please clean up your office, Mr. Bane. I seriously doubt that there will be any reason why the trustees would need to venture down here to the basement, but President Murray and I may bring a few down here to show them why we need more capital investment in the college's astronomy program."

"Of course, sir," came Wallace's plaintive reply.

"Very well, then," Mortimer Chestnut intoned. "I shall leave you to your, uh, crypt."

After Dr. Chestnut departed, Wallace "the Mole" Bane stood frozen in shock. As if it weren't horrifying enough that Dr. Chestnut had effectively relegated him to the role of observatory custodian to get everything in "tip-top" shape. Oh no, now that astro-amateur, Clay Arnold, would be coming to HIS observatory to receive an honorary PhD "How lovely."

Wallace Bane let out a shriek of pain like a primal beast. "It's bad enough that Clay Arnold won the gold medallion that should have been mine! Oh no, now he's coming to get an honorary doctorate from my university! Everyone gets to be called doctor, but me!"

Through teary eyes, Wallace Bane looked around his "crypt". He tried to compose himself, but twenty-five years of professional degradation had finally caught up to him.

"Oh, don't worry, Dr. Chestnut, the Von Timm Observatory will be spotless and the telescope will be ready for use," Wallace muttered aloud. And then he gazed at the picture of Clay Arnold and Maggie Bodine, and the germ of an idea came to him. "Yes, indeed, Dr. Chestnut, we must be prepared for Mr. Arnold and his lovely Ms. Bodine! Yes, indeed, sir, we must make plans!

Chapter 3

AWAKENED EARLY WITH a very heavy heart. I was relieved to see that the heaviness came from Satchmo sitting on my chest rather than a cardiac episode. Thank goodness he hadn't delivered another one of his lifeless furry gifts.

"Okay, you big rodent-whacking beast. Get off my chest. I need to meet Weed and Mace in a few minutes."

Satchmo rubbed his purring face against my nose and took his sweet time ambling off of my chest. Before my feet had a chance to hit the floor, my phone rang. I saw that it was Maggie calling,

and I lay my head back down to reconnect with the woman I love.

"Good morning, handsome!" came the sweet words from my auburn-haired beauty. "Are you ready to dazzle the world with your brilliance today?"

"And good morning to you, too, darling. I was going to call you last night, but Weed left my place after midnight, and I didn't want to disturb your sleep. How are things in Santa Fe?"

"Things are good, busy. That's why I'm up so early. Well that, plus I also just wanted to hear your voice. I've gotten two more promotional projects under contract and that keeps me from thinking about you all the time, Clay. Not that that's a bad thing mind you, but I'm really excited about helping our galleries on Canyon Road promote their clients' artwork."

"I get it," I acknowledged. "We artists can use all of the help we can get, and you're the best! So, what else is going on?"

"Well, I've been talking with my sister, Rita, about some vacation plans that she and Tom are talking about to celebrate their fifteenth wedding anniversary. Originally, they were thinking about taking their daughter, Laura, along with them, but I suggested that I take Laura on a girls' trip so that she and Tom could enjoy some rare alone time together.

Rita really thought it was a great idea. Laura likes the idea, too, and now we just have to decide where we'd like to go. Any suggestions, Clay?"

I thought for a moment and said, "I do have a suggestion. You may not be interested in this because it's not really a vacation, but I just was contacted about something really special that's being given to me in Greencastle, Indiana. I was thinking maybe you and Laura might enjoy joining me and my friends."

"Well, you're right. I never would've thought of Greencastle as a vacation destination but tell me more. And, Clay, please also bear in mind that what a precocious fourteen-year-old girl finds fun could be light-years different than what old fogies like you and me do."

"Right," I agreed. "Anyway, a couple of days ago I received a call from Dr. Hannibal Murray who is the president of Kissinger College in Greencastle which is about ninety minutes away from our home. It's an excellent school, and the town has a fun, vibrant downtown. The whole community has really become a regional music mecca."

"So, in light of my photographic career and recently receiving the Astrophotographer of the Year Award, Kissinger College wants to confer an honorary doctorate on me early next month when school resumes. It's quite an honor and a real surprise, and I've accepted their invitation. Maggie, I was thinking maybe you and Laura might like to come for those festivities and hang with all of us at my place for a few days."

"Wow!" Maggie exclaimed with delight. "Clay, that is awesome. I am so proud of you. An honorary doctorate! Will I have to call you Doctor Arnold now? Please give me the dates that you're thinking of, and I'll discuss it with Laura and Rita and Tom. This could be a very cool trip, not only to celebrate your terrific recognition, but also for Laura to visit Kissinger College and maybe begin thinking about her own college career. I love the idea!"

"Thanks, Maggie, I was hoping you might see it that way. I promise that with Tori, Weed, Mace, and Rennie around, Laura will be well entertained . . . and supervised. Hopefully enough so that you and I can spend some alone time together."

"Oh, that goes without saying!" Maggie replied. "Give me a day or so and I'll get back to you once everyone on my end has had a chance to talk, okay?"

Maggie and I talked a little bit more, mostly about how much we missed each other, and then I told her that there was something important that I wanted to discuss with her, but at the right time and definitely not over the phone. Of course, she didn't know what I was referring to and became concerned. I assured her that it could wait, and to please not worry, but I don't think I did a very good job of assuaging her concerns. I probably shouldn't have said anything until the right time, but I guess I wanted to force myself to begin a difficult conversation.

"Okay, darlin', I have to meet Mace and Weed in ten minutes, and I haven't even crawled out of bed yet. I love you and miss you, and we'll talk really soon."

"Okay, Clay, but please promise me everything is solid between us," Maggie said softly.

"I adore you, Maggie Bodine. I'm sorry I've worried you. Everything is rock solid with us. I promise."

We hung up, and I lay motionless in bed for a few minutes longer thinking about secrets and the heavy burdens they bring. So, in my attempt to lessen my burden by beginning to be more forthright with Maggie about my being an avenging vigilante, I now unintentionally transferred some of that burden to her. Damn!

Ten minutes later I had shaved and cleaned up and was walking across the cobblestone courtyard to meet Mace and Weed for our breakfast at Stella's Diner.

To me, Mace Davis is a giant of a man. Not just because of his imposing physical stature, but mainly because of the strength of his character. At the age of 71, Mace is still a vital, hard-bodied man, capable of handling tough physical labor, and he proves it every day by keeping the buildings within our brewery complex in fine working shape. Mace is also a very devoted friend and a clever problem-solver which came in especially handy about nine months ago when he saved our lives from Clement Hacker's violent attack here at our home.

He has lived on our property ever since arriving from Grand Bahama Island at the age of twelve. When he settled here, the Block Brothers Brewing Company, which was started in 1855, had already gone out of business. The brewery then became the home of the Jeffries Woodworking Mill. Mace worked and lived at the mill for over fifty years until the Jeffries family sold the property to me some seven years ago. The sale of the property to me had one major proviso, that Mace Davis be allowed to live in the complex's old power plant as long as he wished. I agreed and have since felt it was one of the best decisions I ever made. We owe our lives to Mace.

"G'morning guys!" I hailed to Weed and Mace. "Are you ready to hit the road or do you need a few minutes yet?"

"We're good to go," Mace replied. "Rennie has already had his breakfast, and he and Tori are preparing to work in the vegetable garden before it gets too hot. After that they'll work on some of Rennie's homeschool assignments."

"That lad has sure come a long way in the year that he has lived with us," Mace added. "I shudder to think where he'd be today if you hadn't offered him a place to stay instead of that decrepit shack where he lived in south Indy. Having survived on the streets by myself as a kid, I know how dangerous and bleak life can be without a family or friends."

"Well, those days are behind him," I said with relief. "It's great that he has Tori to help educate him and all of us to keep an eye on him, especially you, Mace."

Tori is Weed's sister, and the two of them live in the original Block brothers farmhouse which they built in 1855. Tori has been blind since birth, but that hasn't stopped her from developing into a beautiful woman who has a singing voice like an angel. She and Weed have toured all over the Midwest as a Blues/Jazz duo and are usually greeted by thunderous applause. They are also regular musicians at Stella's Diner and always perform to packed houses.

Rennie Cotton's story is equally dramatic. A number of years ago I was doing a photo-essay in the depressed streets of southern Indianapolis when I took a picture of a very young Rennie sitting alone in the shadowed doorway of an old tenement building. The picture became one of my all-time favorites. About a year ago Mace and I returned to that location to see if we could learn what happened to Rennie.

Long story short: We did find him, but his life was hardly a charmed existence. He had somehow managed to feed himself and evade the authorities, but he was filthy and suffering from malnutrition. With some coaxing and the promise of gainful employment, Rennie reluctantly came to work at the brewery complex. Truth is, he saved Tori and our dog, Lex, when they were attacked while hiking along the White River by Clement Hacker's recalcitrant sons, Newt and Twit. Ever since then, Rennie has been a bona fide member of our "family."

"Hey guys, we're burning daylight!" Weed declared. "I've been thinking about breakfast at Stella's ever since Clay suggested it last night."

A few moments later the three of us piled into my silver Tacoma and were on our way to see Stella and enjoy the unique ambience of her famous diner.

Chapter 4

PULLING INTO THE parking lot at Stella's Diner brought back a flood of emotions. As much as we all love the Diner, it was here that Newt and Twit Hacker attacked several patrons, resulting in our friend, Trent Reynolds, being shot. Fortunately Trent survived, and he played a key role in finally tracking down the Hacker men.

Trent Reynolds is a lifelong friend of mine, and he also went through elementary and high school with Tori and Weed. The three of us weren't especially close with Trent in our school days, but we've all become much closer having survived the violent attacks by the Hacker family last year. Our pal, Trent,

also happens to be the Assistant Superintendent of the Indiana State Police.

"Check it out!" Weed declared. "If I'm not mistaken that's Trent's unmarked government car parked over there. It'll be good to see him. It's been a while."

"Too long," Mace and I said almost simultaneously.

And there at the entrance to the diner, standing in full pulchritude and exotic ensemble, was Stella herself. She was decked out in Leopard tights and a purple and orange top. Quite a spectacle!

"Howdy, boys!" came Stella's full-throated greeting. "I was wondering when you fellas were gonna come see me!" She gave each of us a warm hug and led us into her famous place of business.

"How y'all doing? And Mace, it's been a while since I've seen your smiling face. Where you been?!"

"Same place I always am, Stella . . . minding home and hearth while Tori, Weed and Clay go off carousing."

"C'mere you big lug and give me another hug," Stella commanded to Mace. "And, don't you dare stay gone so long next time, or I swear I'll come hunting for you," Stella said in only half jest.

"Yes, ma'am," Mace replied sheepishly. "I've missed you too, Stella."

Stella led us to a table, gave us some menus, and said that Abby would be over in just a moment to bring us coffee and take our orders.

"By the way, Stella," I said, "We thought we saw Trent Reynolds's car in the parking lot. Is he around?"

Before Stella could respond, we heard an authoritative voice from behind us say, "Yes, I'm around, and I have you three juvenile delinquents in my crosshairs."

We all stood up to greet Trent, who had a broad smile on his face, and Stella took her leave to work the cash register.

"Hey, Trent, it's great to see you!" I said. "You got time for a cup of coffee?"

"Just barely," he replied. "I do need to get back soon, but since you guys were the ones who averted even greater death and destruction last Thanksgiving, sure, I've got time for a cup."

Trent took the chair next to Weed, and the two of them gave each other a knowing nod. Both men had suffered gunshot wounds from Twit Hacker and managed to survive it.

"Brother Reynolds," Weed said to Trent. "How's the shoulder doing? Do you have full range of motion yet, Trent?"

"Not yet," Trent replied stoically. "But as you know, Brother Rawlins, getting shot at point blank range isn't something too many people can recover from. How's your hand?"

Weed held up his hand, and you could see some serious scarring from a bullet that went through the meat of his right hand.

"Well, it is what it is," Weed acknowledged. "As long as I can hold a harmonica, I'm okay with it."

I shivered when I thought back to last Thanksgiving when Twit Hacker rammed his pickup truck into the main entrance of Conner Prairie Hospital, and Weed heroically jumped on the truck's running board to try and stop him. He grabbed the muzzle of Twit's gun and got a bullet through his hand for his efforts.

Just then Abby appeared with a pot of coffee and to take our order. "Hi guys, I see you brought our international celebrity, Clay Arnold, with you."

"Oh?! Trent interjected. "And what has he done now?

"He was recently selected as the Astro-photographer of the Year by Space and Beyond magazine," Abby reported.

Trent raised his eyebrows in proud surprise. And Weed commented, "Oh, it gets even better. Now Kissinger College in Greencastle wants to bestow an honorary doctorate on him for his many artistic achievements. We're all going for the festivities next month. You two care to join us?"

Trent and Abby had been dating ever since the horrific events last Thanksgiving, and they looked at each other. "We'd love to," said Trent, "but let me double-check my calendar, and we'll let you know for sure." Abby echoed that sentiment. As a journalist by training, Abby knew how prestigious Clay's recent recognitions are and said, "We'll be there, Clay." She glanced at Trent and said, "I'll make sure of it." Trent shrugged in mock surrender. "Dr. Clay Arnold, huh?" Trent said. "Who would've guessed it back in eighth grade? I can't wait to tell all of those high-and-mighty professors at the college that I knew you when you had zits!"

"Gee thanks, Mr. ISP Assistant Superintendent," I retorted. "Let's see if we can go somewhere without one of us getting shot."

"Amen to that," Mace said, and he held his coffee cup up to offer a toast.

A few moments later Abby scurried off to take care of other customers, and Trent Reynolds took his leave to help keep Indiana safe for democracy. The three remaining friends enjoyed a leisurely breakfast, and each in his own private way wondered what kind of drama waited down the road.

"So, Clay," Weed began. "We haven't talked much recently about the weapons you had Mace and me fabricate. Are you taking a break from evening the score with bad dudes out there?"

"Well, honestly, I'm not exactly sure," I replied. "I guess the passage of time brings perspective, and while I have no regrets about having 'removed' certain people from the ranks of the living, I must admit to feeling a little less motivated to execute right-wing racist bastards. Don't get me wrong. My blood still boils when I think about Jennifer's murder or see Nazi symbols and Confederate battle flags. Now with Maggie in my life, and frankly all of you, I prefer to focus more on the positive aspects of life rather than being a righter of wrongs. Bottom line is that it's become much harder for me to square being a great partner with Maggie and a respectable friend with all of you if I am hell bent on killing people, even if they truly deserve it."

"Clay, I think Mace and I understand where you're coming from, and we hope you know that we're here to support you no matter what you decide. In the meantime what would you like us to do with the weapons we created?"

The weapons that Weed was referring to were actually high-tech killing devices that Weed and Mace fabricated from spare parts of very old detective-style cameras in my antique camera museum.

"Well, I'm not sure. For now, why don't we just keep them locked away in the subbasement work-shop at home. Perhaps, adopting a more genteel lifestyle is in order at this point in my life anyway."

Mace and Weed nodded their understanding, but they knew that only time would tell . . .

Chapter 5

Dr. Mortimer Chestnut stared out of his office window in the Kurtzmann Science Center on Kissinger College's main campus. He was deep in thought. Formally, Dr. Chestnut was known as the Judge Thaddeus Nathan Professor of Astronomy, and he sat in an endowed chair that was created when Judge Nathan left a major bequest to the college upon his death some twenty years earlier.

Dr. Chestnut never knew Judge Nathan since he joined the college's faculty a few years after the judge passed away. He was well aware that, even to this day, the maturely-aged folks of Greencastle and the college faculty recalled the judge's legendary

life and times with admiration. He was revered as an honorable jurist and community leader and as a highly competent astronomer and philanthropist.

Frankly none of Judge Nathan's history meant a whit to Mortimer Chestnut. All he truly cared about was his academic fiefdom, which also included the Von Timm Observatory and the hefty financial budget that he controlled as department chair.

But Mortimer also had ambitions beyond his department. He knew it was a matter of time, perhaps a year, before President Murray announced his retirement. Mortimer wanted to ascend to that lofty position, but he knew he needed a plan to brighten his professional star. But how to promote his ambitious agenda with the college's board of trustees without appearing like he was drooling? Ah, stealth, cunning, and misdirection. And then he would swoop in to save the day as a noble, selfless hero. Dr. Mortimer Chestnut stared out of his office window and began to hatch a plan. A few minutes later he heard a timid rap on his office door.

"Enter," he declared officiously. "Come, come!"

Mortimer's secretary, Clarabelle Meemo, cautiously pointed her face through the door. "Dr. Chestnut, President Murray called you about twenty minutes ago and asked that you call him before you leave for the day."

"Well, why didn't you let me know he was on the phone?" Mortimer bellowed at poor Clarabelle.

"Well, sir, you told me you didn't want to be disturbed under any circumstances so I took you at your word."

"So, did the old coot say what he wanted?" Dr. Chestnut inquired.

"No, sir, he did not, and I don't think it's appropriate for you to speak about the President of the College with such language . . . sir. He also wanted to know where you were."

"And what did you tell him, Ms. Meemo?"

"Well, I felt awful fibbing to President Murray, so I told him that I didn't have a clue."

"Aaarrggghhh!" Mortimer bellowed. "Very well then, get him back on the phone for me," he commanded.

What Mortimer Chestnut did not know was that Clarabelle Meemo was President Murray's niece, and she had always had a very respectful opinion of her uncle, the president. The other thing about Clarabelle that Dr. Chestnut did not know was that she absolutely detested her bombastic, self-absorbed boss.

Five minutes passed, and Ms. Meemo buzzed Mortimer's office to let him know President Murray was on the line.

"Ah, President Murray, what a delightful surprise. It is wonderful to hear your voice. How may I be of service?"

"All right, cut the phony crap, Mortimer, I'm calling you about your department's role with our upcoming board of trustees meeting and specifically our bestowing the honorary doctorate on Clay Arnold."

Mortimer cringed a bit with the president speaking so directly at him, but he managed to compose himself. "Well, as department chairman, I am certainly looking forward to conferring the award on Mr. Arnold personally at the ceremony."

"Well, guess again, Mortimer, that's not happening! I have someone special in mind for that role, and you're not him," President Murray stated without any equivocation.

Mortimer Chestnut's face turned purple with embarrassment and rage. Clarabelle Meemo had left her speaker phone on so she could eavesdrop on the conversation and had the pleasure of hearing her boss become emotionally unhinged as she locked her desk drawer and quietly departed for the day.

"But, sir!" Mortimer implored the president, "Surely, I am . . ." Alas, Dr. Chestnut was not able to finish his plea as President Murray barreled on with the purpose of his phone call.

"Here's the way it's going to be, Dr. Chestnut. As I believe you may know, Judge Thaddeus Nathan endowed your position within the Astronomy department. Over twenty years ago, Judge Nathan befriended a young neighbor named Wade Henry when a local lunatic killed the judge's wife and Wade Henry's father in the same assault. Afterward the judge became like a father to the young man, and he introduced Wade to the wonders of astronomy."

"Uh, excuse me, sir," Mortimer managed to interject. "Are we talking about THE Wade Henry? The Director of the Galileo Institute for Advanced Astrophysics?"

"Well, of course we are, Mortimer. I suppose you didn't know that Wade Henry grew up near Greencastle on Brick Chapel Road, and both of his parents served admirably on the College's executive staff."

Mortimer Chestnut gulped as he realized that any counter argument that he might offer was utterly fruitless.

"So, here's how it's going to happen: Wade Henry, along with his family, will be present for the award ceremony which he has requested to occur at the Von Timm Observatory. Years ago Judge Nathan and Wade Henry spent many a summer evening peering through our Clark telescope. They even travelled together to Jasper, Alberta, to photograph the dark skies in Canada. Dr. Henry has agreed to confer the doctorate on Clay Arnold and to speak for a few minutes. Afterward we'll have a nice reception at the observatory."

"Yes, sir," Mortimer managed to say. "I have already alerted my staff about the honorary doctorate. Mr. Bane has been instructed to have the grounds and telescope in tip-top shape, and . . ."

That was as far as Mortimer got. "Look here, Chestnut, I want everything perfect for this, and I am holding you personally responsible. All of these people and their guests are very important to Kissinger College. Is that clear? I'll have my assistant talk with Ms. Meemo to make certain everything is seamless. Oh, and another thing, Dr. Chestnut, the next time I call you, I expect you to be available, or to at least leave word with Ms. Meemo of your whereabouts. Is that understood?"

Mortimer Chestnut sputtered and began to reply, but it was too late. President Murray had already hung up. He strutted and fretted around his office muttering to himself. "That old codger of a president can't retire soon enough to suit me! I must create a carefully composed strategy for the observatory reception for Clay Arnold. Something with cunning and misdirection. But what and who can I implicate so in the end I can swoop in and become the hero? Perhaps even Wade Henry might be impressed with my clever skills."

Mortimer returned to his desk a little calmer. He idly scanned his faculty directory, and a small smile came to his face when he saw one name in particular, Mister Wallace "The Mole" Bane.

"Tip-top idea", Mortimer Chestnut said out loud to himself. "Tip-top indeed."

Chapter 6

MACE, WEED, AND I arrived home from Stella's Diner around 10:00 a.m. after reconnecting with old friends and satiating ourselves on the diner's great grub. The three of us agreed we'd meet around eleven thirty in the subbasement workshop after taking care of our personal chores. For Mace that meant making certain the power plant was working efficiently and that good ol' Lex had plenty to eat and a chance to get some exercise. Lex is our three-legged, black Labrador Retriever who took a bullet trying to save Tori from an attack by Newt and Twit Hacker a year ago. Lex is a hero in our eyes, and all of us do what we can to make his life a little easier.

Weed went back to the farmhouse to check in with Tori and Rennie who were still working in the garden, and I went upstairs to my home office to check for messages, and to put some finishing touches on a recent photography assignment using Lightroom. I saw that I had an e-mail waiting for me from my agent, Lily Deupree, and several from friends and colleagues congratulating me on my recent award from *Space and Beyond* magazine.

Lily's message provided updates to my travel schedule confirming she had successfully booked a photo assignment for me in Moab, Utah, next week and on the NASA Today television show in early October about my being named Astrophotographer of the Year. I hadn't had an opportunity yet to tell Lily about receiving Kissinger College's honorary doctorate next month, and fortunately the dates she gave me wouldn't interfere with my trip to Greencastle plus the extra few days that Maggie and her niece, Laura, might be spending here with us. I wrote Lily back and made sure that she was aware of commitments on my end.

Since I still had an hour or so before I met with Mace and Weed, I turned off the lights in my office, lowered the window blinds, and focused on an image on my computer screen. A client had requested a 30" × 45" aluminum print of the Milky Way that had won the gold medallion for me, and I wanted to make certain that it still met my artistic standards. In my Lightroom program I made a few very minor adjustments to the image's color temperature, clarity, and vibrance, all of which provided the improvements I wanted. I was just about to shut my computer down when I saw a new message appear from an unknown sender: *"So, Mr. World-Famous Astrophotographer, you think you are so good with a camera, yes?! Let's see how you are at solving problems . . . stay tuned . . ."*

I wasn't sure what it meant and chose not to immediately reply. While it wasn't unusual for me to receive messages from folks I didn't know, this message seemed to have a bit of a nefarious ring to it, and it left me feeling unsettled. I turned off my computer and headed for my home elevator that would take me down three floors to my sub-basement workshop. All the way down a suspicion niggled at the back of my mind that this would not be the last I heard from this unknown sender.

Weed and Mace were already waiting for me when I entered the subterranean workshop. Originally, this space had been constructed by the Block brothers to store kegs of beer, but in recent months it had become a clandestine laboratory of sorts for Weed and Mace to design, fabricate, and test stealthy weapons for my use in evening the score with the nastier elements of society. The workshop also had an entrance to a secret passageway that ran under the courtyard and connected it to a shed just behind Tori and Weed's farmhouse. Had it not been for Mace's knowledge of that hidden passageway, Tori, Rennie, and I would likely have been killed by Clement Hacker nine months ago.

As I approached Weed and Mace, they were hunched over a work bench examining one of my antique detective cameras and having a lively conversation.

Maurice "Weed" Rawlins didn't start his career as a Blues and Jazz musician. He attended MIT for college and graduate school, and developed such a great penchant for blowing things up that the Defense Department brass was salivating to get their hands on him. It wasn't meant to be; however, since Weed didn't care for the buttoned-down life. Regardless, when I needed some help weaponizing some of my antique cameras, it was like riding a bicycle again for him.

Then there was Mace who had no formal education and relied solely on his intuition and skill to copy some of the lethal devices Weed devised. Mace had studied Weed's notes and created a particularly deadly stun weapon from an antique camera called the "Demon". The Demon was originally introduced in 1889 by the American Camera Company. It was a popular camera because it was small and therefore useful in capturing candid pictures. When Mace got his hands on it, the camera went from being an old camera to a highly charged electricity emitter that sent out blue streams of voltage to any target within ten feet. It was the device that Mace used to take out Clement Hacker as he prepared to kill us. Weed and Mace formed a great team, and they used the subterranean workshop to create several weapons that I used as an avenging vigilante.

"Wow, Mace!" Weed exclaimed. "I am very impressed by how you converted the good ol' Demon into such a powerful device."

"Well, you shouldn't be that impressed, Weed. I was pretty much following your designs for other weapons," Mace replied.

"I can see that you two have been having a lot of fun down here," I exclaimed. "Can we set up a target and see how the Demon performs now that it's fully charged?"

Mace set up a paper target of a human form on the wall and instructed me to stand about eight feet away. "Like the original Kodak ads used to read, 'You press the button and we do the rest.'"

I did as Mace instructed, and a cobalt-blue charge of electricity shot out from the Demon and utterly consumed the paper target in a matter of seconds. Weed let out a low whistle of admiration. The three of us looked at each other and grinned and guffawed like high school boys.

"I think we have a winner, guys!" I said. "How long does it take to recharge?" I asked.

"Probably no more than fifteen minutes even if it's been fully discharged," Mace offered, and Weed nodded his agreement.

I told them that my agent, Lily, had notified me a little earlier that I had an assignment in Moab, Utah, in two days, and that I'd like to take the Demon with me, just in case someone misbehaves.

Mace and Weed looked at me and wondered out loud about my thoughts of cutting back on my avenging ways.

"Just because I take the Demon with me, doesn't mean that I'll use it," I said seriously. "On the other hand . . ." I let those words hang in the air.

The three of us rummaged around in the sub-basement workshop for a few minutes longer pondering designs for some of my other antique detective cameras. I flashed on Maggie momentarily and again felt the burden of my secrets. I briefly looked at the ceiling and saw remnants of smoke from the burned target and wondered how I would ever be able to tell her the truth without losing her.

Several minutes later the three of us wrapped up our shenanigans in the workshop and were walking across the courtyard toward the farmhouse when

Rennie came running out to greet us. He had a basket full of tomatoes, peppers, kale, and beans that he and Tori had picked from the garden that morning.

"Wow, Rennie, you look like the Jolly Green Giant with all of those veggies," I said.

"Jolly Green who?" Rennie replied.

"You know, the big green guy who says, 'ho, ho, ho' and pushes a lot of vegetables on people," Weed added.

Rennie looked at him like he was from another planet.

"Okay," Weed said in mock surrender. "Must be a generational thing like Howdy Doody and hula hoops."

Rennie said, "You're funny, Weed," and he walked back inside the farmhouse to help Tori prepare lunch.

We followed Rennie inside and were immediately treated to the soothing sound of Tori's singing voice and the aroma of her cooking wafting from the kitchen.

"From the sounds of those footsteps, it sounds like we have three hungry men looking for an easy meal," she playfully chided. "So if you want to eat anytime soon, I suggest you wash your hands, help set the table, and take drink orders."

Mace, Weed, and I followed her marching orders, and within a few minutes, we were all seated at the kitchen table and ready to chow down. I took my time glancing around the table at each person as they filled their plate and carried on with friendly banter. This is my family, I thought to myself, with the absence of Maggie, of course. I want each of them to be safe and happy and ultimately to be proud of me as a friend they can rely on.

Tori's voice brought me back. "So, Clay, where are you off to next? You surely have something else coming up."

"I do," I admitted and went on to tell her and Rennie about my receiving an honorary doctorate from Kissinger College. "Weed and Mace are coming and Trent and Abby, too. I sure hope you and Rennie will be there."

"Well, congratulations, Clay! My goodness, aren't you full of surprises?! Of course we'll be there, won't we, Rennie?!"

"I thought you're a photographer, Clay," Rennie stated. "Why do you want to be a doctor with all of that blood and needles and stuff?"

That got a hearty round of laughter from everyone, and Weed tried to explain that it's a different kind of doctor.

"Okay," Rennie continued. "If there's no blood and needles, I'll definitely be there! Will there be food?"

"All you can eat," Clay assuaged. "There's a very good chance that Maggie and her niece, Laura, will be there, too and probably staying here for a few days afterward."

"It'll be a great time, I'm sure, and I'm pleased I'll have other women to talk with for a change," Tori admitted.

I explained the dates and schedule of events that Dr. Murray told me.

"And, my agent, Lily, just informed me that I have a new photography assignment in the parks around Moab, Utah, in two days. I know it's short notice, but I was thinking maybe Rennie could join me and be my helper."

"Seriously!" Rennie shouted as he shot imploring glances toward Tori and Mace. "Can I go? And where's Utah? They don't have any jolly green giants there, do they?"

"Actually, it's pretty good timing, and no they don't have any any jolly green giants," Tori said. "Weed and I have to prepare for a big show at Stella's Diner this coming weekend, and we could use the time while you're gone to rehearse. Don't worry, Clay, I'll have Mr. Rennie Cotton all spiffed up, packed, and ready to go."

"Mace, can you do without Rennie's help for a few days?" I asked.

"It'll be tough, but I reckon so," he confirmed. "Have a great time, guys, and don't go falling off any cliffs, or get bitten by rattlesnakes, or get swept away by flash floods, or eaten by coyotes, or . . ."

Rennie's eyes initially went wide with fright and then he relaxed when he saw everyone laughing.

"So, it's settled then," Clay said. I'll text Lily and ask her to make flight and hotel accommodations for two gentlemen travelers off to see the world! But remember, Rennie, we're there to work, okay?"

"Yessir, you know I'll work hard, Clay."

"I know you will, Rennie," I replied. "And I promise we'll have a good time, too. It won't be all work. It's also about time you started to learn more about photography; not just mastering the equipment but training your eyes, too. So if you like, I'll be happy to teach you a few things, too." Rennie enthusiastically nodded his agreement.

We finished our lunch, cleaned up the kitchen, and went our separate ways. Mace and Lex headed back to the power plant presumably for well-earned naps. Weed said he had errands in town which he used as an excuse to visit a lady friend. Rennie and Tori cleared the kitchen table and spread out Rennie's school books, and I headed back home to prepare for my photo shoot in Moab. As I crossed the courtyard, Satchmo materialized from out of nowhere.

"C'mon, you furry beast. You can help me get ready."

We went to my office, and when I sat down at my computer, I saw that I had a message come in from Maggie confirming that she and Laura would be coming to Indiana.

"Better yet," I said to Satchmo, "maybe you can help me figure out a way to come clean with Maggie without screwing up both of our lives."

Satchmo stretched, looked in my direction, and then bounded away to continue his critter surveillance of the brewery complex.

"I guess I'm on my own with this one, huh?"

Chapter 7

WALLACE BANE MUTTERED to himself as he put a fresh coat of paint on the entrance to the Von Timm Observatory. He couldn't decide who he wanted to curse more, Clay Arnold or his boss, Dr. Mortimer Chestnut. So, he cursed them both.

Earlier that day Dr. Chestnut had called Wallace with a lengthy list of projects he wanted the Mole to conclude prior to the board of trustees' visit in ten days.

"I need you to power wash the concrete patio all around the observatory perimeter and paint the entrance, inside and out. You need to contact facilities management and have them set up tables and

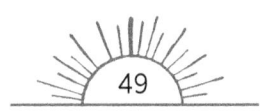

seating for seventy-five people. Oh, and have them install a canopy over everything in case it rains."

"But Dr. Chestnut," Wallace moaned, "can't you ask Ms. Meemo to handle some of those details?"

"Of course I can," Dr. Chestnut snapped, "but I'm asking you, aren't I?"

Chestnut continued, "And I need you to make certain that the bathroom is scrubbed inside and out. It needs to be in tip-top shape! Tip-top! And while you're at it, clean up that hovel that you call an office, including your sink and toilet, too. Oh, and put something up to hide the entrance to that creepy storage area. No telling where we'll bring these trustees, and I don't even mind them seeing most of your crypt if it'll help free up some more cash for my department."

"Is that all, sir?" Wallace the Mole managed to squeak out.

"Oh, and ask Dr. South to give you a hand cleaning and calibrating the optics on the Clark telescope. I certainly wouldn't expect someone with only a master's degree to be able to do that unsupervised," Mortimer stabbed.

"Of course, sir. Oh, I understand that Dr. Wade Henry will be returning to Greencastle to confer the honorary doctorate on Clay Arnold, sir," Wallace said.

Mortimer Chestnut's voice grew grave, and he replied, "Yes, he is. What of it?!"

"Nothing sir. I just thought that a man of your position might've enjoyed that honor . . . sir," Wallace successfully lobbed back at him.

"Don't worry yourself about such matters, Mr. Bane. In any event I plan to take a much-deserved vacation as soon as the ceremony is over," Dr. Chestnut informed. "Remember now! Tip-top! Everything must be tip-top!"

That was four hours ago. Now, Wallace had completed perhaps only 10 percent of the projects his draconian boss had assigned. He roughly brushed gray paint on the interior of the entrance, but with each stroke he managed to slow his angry motion as he began to review his surreptitious plans for the reception.

"Thank goodness, I have time to get everything completed," he murmured aloud, "both for my boss . . . and for myself."

Wallace labored for the duration of the afternoon, and as the sun began to set, he heard the sound of tires crunching the gravel in the observatory's parking lot. Fearing that Dr. Chestnut had returned, he hid behind the front door. A moment later he heard a car door close and the light tread of footsteps on gravel. To Wallace's total shock, Clarabelle Meemo appeared in the doorway.

"Ms. Meemo!" Wallace stammered. "What are you doing here? I mean is something wrong? Did Dr. Chestnut send you with more assignments for me?"

Clarabelle couldn't help but smile at Wallace's discomfiture. She didn't know him well, but she had a feeling that they both shared an extreme dislike of their boss.

"Relax, Mr. Bane, I am not here to add to your workload. In fact, I heard all of the lengthy instructions Dr. Chestnut gave you over the phone and thought that perhaps I might be able to help lighten your load."

Wallace Bane was stunned. Very few people at the College even knew he existed, let alone ever reached out to him in any helpful way.

"But I don't understand," Wallace replied cautiously. "With Dr. Chestnut as your boss, I just assume that you're here at his behest."

"I understand why you would be so suspicious, Mr. Bane, but I assure you that I'm here to help," Clarabelle assuaged. "Now let's take a look at your work list and get cracking!"

Over the next few hours, Wallace and Clarabelle plowed through one clean-up project after another until exhaustion overtook both of them. What she hadn't told Wallace was that she had kept her uncle, President Murray, informed of Dr. Chestnut's relentless abuse of Wallace Bane . . . and others. He had encouraged her to be of whatever assistance she deemed most useful.

"I can come back tomorrow after work, too, Mr. Bane, but let's keep my assistance as our little secret. No reason to get Dr. Chestnut's hackles up any more than they already are," Clarabelle advised.

"Thank you, Ms. Meemo, for your very kind help. I promise to respect your anonymity."

After Ms. Meemo departed, Wallace walked around the observatory inspecting the improvements that he and Clarabelle had made inside and out. He was impressed by their progress but still remained a little incredulous as to why Ms. Meemo would want to help him. "It's just so surprising!" he heard himself say aloud. "Why me?"

———

Meanwhile out in the hinterlands of Putnam county, an old panel truck rumbled down County Road 250 North past the Wurster Tree Farm and came to a stop about a mile later. Dr. Mortimer Chestnut got out and walked to a metal gate that secured the entrance to an obscure lane. He unlocked the padlock and pulled his vehicle inside the tree-lined lane and relocked the gate behind him. He killed his headlights and waited a full three minutes in the darkness listening for any sounds of passersby. Aside from the hoots of a pair of owls and the wind in the pines, it was quiet. He turned on his parking lights and continued down the lane for another hundred yards and came to a stop at an old cabin that lay hidden beneath a canopy of locust trees. This was Mortimer's secluded getaway, his escape from lesser people and the tedium of the college.

Mortimer went to the rear of the panel truck and pulled out two large containers of nonperishable supplies. There were enough to last him for an extended stay. He lugged them into the cabin and situated them neatly in the kitchen cabinets. He then returned to the truck for a cache of electronic surveillance equipment and a .22 caliber hand gun that he kept for personal defense. He decided to keep his stun gun and pepper spray in his truck for future use. It was all part of an evolving plan that Mortimer was still concocting. Once Mortimer installed the surveillance cameras around the perimeter of his cabin, he returned inside to check their function on his video monitor. Everything worked as it should.

Lastly, Mortimer went to the lower level of the cabin to inspect a rarely used storage room. He flicked on the light which revealed a windowless stone room with a bare light bulb in the ceiling and a drain in the floor. There was a crude cot in the corner of the room and a stained sink and commode, nothing else.

"Hmmm," Mortimer Chestnut murmured to himself. "This cell should prove most useful. It's certainly not tip-top, but most useful nonetheless."

He returned to the main level of the cabin and gave everything a final look. Then he activated his surveillance equipment, returned to his truck, and headed back toward his home on Seminary Street in Greencastle.

"Hmmm," he murmured to himself again as he drove slowly past Dr. Murray's presidential residence. "President Mortimer Chestnut. It has a very nice ring to it, even if I do say so myself."

Chapter 8

I COULDN'T FIGURE OUT what that strange sound was. My mind drifted somewhere between fitful sleep and a lucid wakefulness that I tried to ignore. Then it dawned on me that the strange sound was my phone, and I fumbled for it on my night table as I tried to force myself back to full consciousness.

"Hello," I managed to mumble.

"And hello to you, too," came Maggie's bright voice. "Did I call you too early?"

"Uh no, I was just getting up," I fibbed. "What time is it?"

"Well, here in Santa Fe it's six thirty, so it must be eight thirty where you are."

"Yikes, I gotta get moving," Clay said finally returning to full lucidity. "How are you, Maggie?"

"I'm doing great," she replied. "and I have very good news for you. Laura and I will be coming to Indiana in a week to celebrate your doctorate and hang out with you while Rita and Tom are on vacation celebrating their anniversary."

"Oh, Maggie, thank you! I can't wait to see you, and I promise we'll all go out of our way to make sure that Laura's trip is memorable. I don't think I told you that I'm going to Moab tomorrow morning for a three-day photo shoot. Rennie's coming with me as my assistant. I thought it was high time that he finally flew in an airplane and got to see a different part of the world that isn't flat and filled with corn and soybeans everywhere you look."

"That sounds like a great learning experience for him, Clay. I admire the way that each of you has taken him under your wing. You've probably saved his life," Maggie added.

"I suppose, maybe," I said. "But he's been there for all of us, too. Honestly, I just feel better about myself for being a friend to a kid in need. Probably the same for Mace, Tori, and Weed, too. He's definitely worth it."

There was a moment of awkward silence, and Clay filled the void by saying, "I know I concerned you the last time we talked. I never wanted to cause you any doubt about us because I am devoted to you. I want to be transparent about my life, past and present, I promise you that we'll have a clarifying conversation when you're here next week."

"Well, I would be lying if I said I hadn't thought much about it," Maggie admitted. "Nature abhors a vacuum and tends to fill it up with all sorts of scenarios."

We switched subjects by my asking about her work and then talking about the different things we could do with Laura around Indianapolis after the festivities in Greencastle are over. And with all of the amenities out of the way, we then toyed with each other with a little mushy phone sex, which while fun, certainly fell short of the real deal. It was clear that both of us were about busting at the seams and could barely wait to reconnect. Oh boy!

The rest of the day was spent in preparation for my trip with Rennie to Moab, Utah. Tori had him all packed and ready to go, and he was very helpful carefully loading my camera gear in the Tacoma. Then the next morning came, and Rennie and I bid adieu to Mace, Tori, and Weed. Rennie was really excited, and I could tell he was a little nervous, too, since he had never flown before or even traveled anywhere outside of central Indiana. We arrived at the Indianapolis airport, and Rennie was speechless in wide-eyed wonder as he saw all of the planes on the tarmac.

"Don't worry, my man!" I said to him. "I've got your back, plus these pilots are really good."

He kept his eyes trained on all of the planes taking off and landing and simply said, "Uh huh."

We boarded our direct flight to Salt Lake City, and I made certain that he had the window seat so he could take everything in. I smiled to myself when his hand firmly latched on to my forearm as the plane taxied down the runway and lifted off.

"Are you okay?" I asked him when we got to cruising altitude. He nodded his head affirmatively and just kept staring at the clouds and the tiny objects on the ground. "Yeah," he finally said. He turned to me and smiled broadly. "Yeah, I'm okay. Thanks, Clay."

When we arrived in the Salt Lake City airport, we collected our gear and walked over to the car rental counter where Lily had reserved a compact car for us.

"How would you feel if we upgraded our choice of vehicles?" I said to Rennie. The rental agent suggested a few other possible cars, and Rennie leaped at the opportunity to rent a Lexus SUV. "Now, we're riding in style!" he exclaimed, and the agent handed him the keys and playfully advised that we keep it out of ditches.

When we settled into the Lexus, Rennie and I took a few minutes to go over the map and entered our destination into the GPS. Instead of taking the I-15 route, we opted for State Route 6 toward Moab. Not only was it more direct, but it also was much more scenic.

"Check it out, Rennie. I figure we have about a four-hour drive to Moab. Why don't we plan on spending the night in Price which is about halfway, and that way we can enjoy a leisurely drive and visit a few sights along the way?"

Rennie's eyes were glued to the foreign-looking landscape all around him, and he voiced a brief, "Uh huh." We drove in silence for a few miles, and Rennie smiled at the amazing sights he was seeing.

"I knew Utah would be cool from the things that Tori and Weed told me, but I had no idea that everything here would be so different from home with the red rocks and the mountains . . . jeez the mountains! Man!"

We drove toward Price and stopped at a few places along the way. I handed Rennie one of my extra cameras, and for the first time, gave him some basic instructions on taking pictures. We set the camera's settings on automatic so he wouldn't get too confused dealing with new concepts. My goal was for him to get comfortable framing pictures in his viewfinder and enjoy snapping away. He took right to it.

I couldn't help but think back to when I was around his age, and my parents gave me my first camera. It changed my life. I also thought back to the first time I met Jennifer Skyler at one of my gallery exhibitions when I was looking at a picture I had taken of Rennie a few years earlier. It was when he was living alone on the streets of Indianapolis. He was an alone little boy sitting in the shadow of a tenement doorway. A lot of time had passed between then and now, and I wondered about the changes that lay ahead for all of us. For now, it was just Rennie and me on the road together, and it gave me a sense of purpose and peace.

We arrived in the town of Price around 8:00 p.m. and managed to find a motel with a restaurant and a room with two queen beds. I sent an e-mail to a chap named Chris Hazeltine who was my contact for the Moab area photoshoot. We agreed that we would meet at noon the next day to map out our project.

"I'm starved!" Rennie declared.

"Well, why don't you check out the restaurant, and I'll meet you there after I get a message off to Lily and organize our gear, probably fifteen minutes."

Rennie shot out of the door and went trotting down the corridor toward the main lobby. He felt alive with wonder. Even after coming to live at Clay's place, Rennie preferred the feeling of security he had at the brewery complex. He didn't care to venture to the big city a lot. He enjoyed his trips with whoever in the family wanted to go to town, but he still liked being at home more. But now he was ready to have fun and do some quick exploring while Clay was busy.

Rennie walked down a well-lit corridor that ran behind the lobby desk. There was a large conference room that was vacant at this hour, but an adjacent meeting room still had twenty or so attendees. He glanced inside and saw a lot of bored and tired-looking people. Rennie walked further down the corridor and came upon the rear service doors to the kitchen. He peered in and saw the kitchen staff still hard at work preparing meals. An Asian cook saw Rennie in the doorway and brought a fortune cookie to him which he eagerly accepted with a smile and a nod.

Rennie continued to walk down the corridor which actually completed a square and brought him close to his point of origin near the main lobby. Ahead he saw a glass wall and the indoor swimming pool beyond.

"Wow, this is amazing!" he chortled. He stepped inside to get a better view and was immediately met with the warm, wet smell of chlorine. The only occupants at this hour were a man and a woman, both in their forties, who seemed very much into each other. Rennie walked inside to look at the diving board and water in the deep end.

A moment later a rough voice hollered at him, "Hey boy, you get your black ass out of here pronto. Nobody wants your kind near the water."

"Golly, easy mister," Rennie said evenly. "I'm not hurting anything. I'm sorry you're mad."

"Yeah, well I get real mad when we can't get our privacy, especially from some little coon kid. Now get on out of here before I come over there and throw you out."

Rennie looked into the man's eyes and just shook his head in disbelief. "Man, you need to go to church or something. Maybe get a little more fiber in your diet."

At that, the man threw his water bottle at Rennie, but his aim was way off. Rennie turned around and exited the pool area door still shaking his head. A few moments later he ran into me by the entrance to the restaurant, and the two of us were shown to a booth. I could tell that something about Rennie's mood wasn't quite right.

"What's up?" I asked. "Back in the room you were busting your buttons to go explore, and now you're acting very subdued."

"Why is it that some people are so mean, Clay? I just don't understand."

"What happened, Rennie?" I asked.

"I wasn't doing anything wrong, Clay. I was just looking around. I went inside the pool area and this man started hollering at me and talking about my black ass and called me a little coon. Then, he threw his water bottle at me. I just left."

My blood was beginning to boil. "Do you think he worked here or was he a guest?"

"I guess he was a guest because he and a woman were in bathing suits. I swear, Clay, I didn't do anything wrong. He was just plain hateful."

I was about to get up and head to our room for the Demon camera that I'd packed when I looked at Rennie's sorrowful face and thought maybe I could turn this into a learning experience . . . for both of us. I stayed seated.

"Look, Rennie, some people just aren't secure enough within themselves, so they have to talk down to others. I'm so sorry it happened. Some people just can't see past skin color. I'm sure this is something you already know. It's painful to be subjected to such ignorance. Fact is you'll probably have to deal with it throughout your life. I will tell you this, though, that the best way for you to rise above this sort of bigotry is to get a really good education and be surrounded by people who care about you for who you are. That's what we're here for. Understand?"

"Yeah, I understand, Clay. It's still not easy." Rennie replied.

I patted Rennie on the shoulder. "C'mon, are you still hungry?" I asked. "I sure am, and it looks like they've got a good menu, too."

"I can eat!" Rennie replied with renewed enthusiasm.

I made a mental note to keep the Demon camera with me but was determined to just talk with the man who was abusive to Rennie if we ran into him again. Maggie's face flashed in my mind, and I felt that I had made the right decision.

We enjoyed our dinner, and Rennie surprised me with a definite curiosity about photography and the camera I loaned him. I must admit that I got a real reminder about how far we've come technologically when he asked me what film was. I felt a little old.

"When we get back home, we should spend some time in my wet darkroom. Digital photography is terrific, but you should also have a sense for what it takes to create great tonal quality in pictures by using dodging and burning. Then once you've mastered that, doing postprocessing of digital images becomes even more second nature."

I could tell I was starting to lose him, so I decided to save the photography discussion for another time. We both finished our meals and agreed it was time to hit the hay. Rennie had been a good traveler all day, and aside from his run-in with the nasty guy at the pool, it had been a pretty good day for two guys on the road. Tomorrow would be another day . . .

Chapter 9

THE NEXT MORNING Rennie and I woke up early and after a quick breakfast, we prepared to drive the final two hours from Price to Moab. Even with doing some sightseeing along the way, we would still have plenty of time to meet our contact, Chris Hazeltine.

"Rennie, why don't you start loading some of our gear in the Lexus while I quickly touch base with Chris. Then stop at the front desk to tell the clerk we'll be checking out in a few minutes. I'll meet you in the lobby, okay?"

Rennie picked up our backpacks and headed off to the parking lot. I sent three text messages: one

to Chris to confirm we'd meet him at noon at the Sunset Inn; another message to Tori to let her know that everything was going fine; and a third mushy message to Maggie to tickle her fancy. Mine, too.

When I got to the lobby, I didn't see Rennie, so I walked outside to see if he needed any help stowing our gear. What I saw sent a wave of fear and rage through me.

A big white man had Rennie pinned against the side of our car and was slobbering racial slurs at him. Rennie was trying to break free, but the man clearly had a size advantage over my young friend. I immediately raced over to try to defuse the confrontation.

"I'm gonna mess you up, you little black prick," I heard the man threaten Rennie. "I didn't get you at the pool, but now your little coon ass is gonna get a whupping." To his credit Rennie took a swing at the man and connected a solid jab to his throat. That only enraged the redneck more, and he reared back to deliver what would be a crippling blow. I grabbed at the man's meaty arm and interrupted his swing. Rennie broke free and scooted behind me.

"Hey, hold on, mister!" I yelled at him. "Ease up! He's just a kid." I told Rennie to go inside and have the desk clerk call the police. He didn't need to be told twice.

"Who the fuck are you?" the assailant snarled. "You want some of this too?"

"I'm that young man's friend is who I am," I said. I tried to diffuse the situation, but my blood was boiling, and I reached inside my pocket to feel for the Demon camera just in case.

"That little darky interrupted me and my girl-friend at the pool last night, and I was gonna teach him a lesson."

"Look mister, he's just a boy, and I'm sure he didn't mean you any trouble," I tried to assuage.

"C'mon, Jerry," his girlfriend urged from a few feet away. "That nigger-lover ain't worth it, especially if the cops show up." She was standing next to their Harley hog, but good ol' Jerry ignored her.

"They're taking over America. Those damn blacks and Mexicans. We gotta make a stand before it's too late," Jerry slobbered at her. "And white guys like this asshole are making it worse."

"Jesus mister, just ease up, will ya?" I tried again, but Jerry felt emboldened by his size advantage over me. He took a lumbering swing at me and landed a glancing blow to my shoulder as I tried to move out of the way. It pushed me back a few steps. Rennie came back outside and stood by our car.

"All right, that's it," I said. "We can do it your way if you want. You or your bike?" I asked evenly.

I pulled the Demon from my pocket and fingered the power button.

"Fuck you," he snarled. "You ain't touching my ride." He reared back to swing at me again.

Time seemed to stand still for a moment. I saw this huge bigot getting ready to slam me. I thought again about Maggie and the secret burdens I feel, and I knew that Rennie would witness how I handled a violent situation. Time seemed to resume its normal speed again, and I pressed the release button on the Demon. A blue charge of angry electricity shot out from the Demon and engulfed the man's Harley. Fortunately for all of us, the chopper didn't explode, but the Harley's electrical system was totally fried into an irreparable smoldering mess.

"My bike!" he bellowed like a wounded child. "You killed my bike!" His complicit girlfriend stood stone still in shock and awe.

"Your choice, mister," I said. "Do you want to quit while you're still able?" I evenly offered.

The brute took a long look at his bike and then at the Demon camera in my hand. It was clear that he really wanted to come at me again, but looking at his devastated Harley took the fight out of him. I slowly backed toward our Lexus and quickly nodded for Rennie to jump inside. He didn't need any more encouragement. I jumped inside, too, and as we pulled away, I saw Jerry and his girlfriend examining the carnage to the Harley and heard the sound of sirens heading in the motel's direction.

"That was awesome!" Rennie shouted as we headed for the highway.

I glanced in the rearview mirror to see if anyone was following us and gave the Lexus some extra gas as we turned onto the entry ramp. "Yeah!" I added. "I doubt that biker thought it was awesome." Rennie saw a small, satisfied smile appear on my face.

We gladly left the town of Price behind us and looked forward to a fresh beginning in the amazing landscapes around Moab.

Rennie and I settled in for the scenic drive southeast toward Moab. We were both silent for a long stretch of time, and after a while I asked Rennie if he needed to talk about what had happened in the parking lot.

"I just don't understand why people are so hateful sometimes," Rennie said for the second time in less than twelve hours. "I mean, I didn't do anything wrong, but that man really wanted to hurt me. I'm just glad you came outside when you did, Clay."

"Me too!" I replied. "We can talk about it as much or as little as you want, Rennie. You're our friend, and we want you to know that we have your back."

"I am curious about that Demon camera thing, though," Rennie said. "Can I get me one of those?"

At that point I felt a stab of guilt rise in me. Not only was I concerned about coming clean with Maggie, but I also was concerned about the life lessons I was instilling in an impressionable young man.

"Probably not," I replied noncommittally. "Besides I'd rather see you shooting things with a camera rather than some lethal device. Eventually, you may even find that using a camera to draw attention to issues can be just as deadly to bad people as using a gun or in our case, the Demon."

I looked over at Rennie and our eyes met. He nodded his head in a way that told me he was beginning to understand. Equally important, I was beginning to feel that my photographic career may have just had a major epiphany. I used to photograph inner-city scenes that drew attention to societal issues. I thought about how I could do even more.

We continued onward in silence for a while, and both of us let our conversation sink in. We observed the changing landscape and that helped separate us from the ugly experience in Price.

Despite the number of times I've been to different areas of Utah, the shapes and colors of the land never cease to fascinate me. For a first-time viewer like Rennie, the landscape took on an almost mystical appearance.

"Wow," Rennie exhaled. "I just thought this was the kind of stuff you only saw in books."

I smiled at his sense of wonder and tried to imagine what it must be like for a ghetto kid to see what Rennie was taking in now. His reaction probably wasn't that much different than how people of white European stock reacted when they first saw these sights a couple of hundred years ago. Awe!

Rennie finally said, "So, I know that we're not seeing the kinds of land and things like we see back home, but it feels like something else is different about it, too."

I was pleased that Rennie had been able to put aside the episode at the motel. "It's the light," I remarked. "It's more radiant, more intense because of the lack of pollution and the dryness in the atmosphere."

"Yeah, I can see that," he replied intuitively.

"For years artists and photographers have ventured out here for that very reason. About a hundred years ago, an artist named Georgia O'Keeffe painted scenes of the land and plant life in the southwest, and it colored my thinking about the variations of light. And for a photographer, it's all about light and how we visually record it."

Rennie vacantly nodded his understanding, but it was clear that he was mesmerized by what he was seeing and paid little attention to my commentary. We continued on until we reached the outskirts of Moab. We saw directional signs for Canyonlands National Park, Dead Horse Point State Park, and, of course, Arches National Park, all within easy driving distance.

We pulled into the parking lot of the Sunset Inn a few minutes before noon, and Chris Hazeltine was already waiting for us in the lobby.

"It is such a pleasure to meet you, Mr. Arnold. We are thrilled that you'll be providing our visitors association with fresh, new images."

"Please call me Clay," I offered. "And this fine young man is my associate, Rennie Cotton."

"It's a pleasure to meet you as well," Chris said warmly. "And I see that you have your camera ready, too."

"Of course!" Rennie replied with pride. "Me and Clay are associates."

While Rennie got us checked in at the front desk and hauled some of our gear to our room, Chris and I went over the specifics of which parks he wanted us to shoot. I suggested that he might consider some images of the Milky Way and the night sky, and he was thrilled at the suggestion. Frankly, I was more excited about taking pictures of the night sky in the parks because a gazillion other photographers have already shot so many great images of the sandstone arches, hoodoos, and canyons in the daytime. Better to be unique, I think. We agreed that I would send him some pictures to review later tomorrow, and that we would meet at the end of our three days around Moab to review more images and talk about next steps in the process.

After Chris left, Rennie and I decided to relax in our room for a while. He was fascinated with the Canon camera I loaned to him and had lots of good questions about focus, f/stops, shutter speeds, ISO, and white balance settings.

"Let's do this," I suggested. "We could both probably use a good nap right now, and then after looking around Moab and having dinner, let's plan on staying out pretty much all evening shooting the night sky. We could head out to Dead Horse Point State Park, and I'll help you get everything set up to take some amazing pictures. I remember a place that should give us great views of the Milky Way with the Colorado River carving its way through canyons one thousand feet below our feet. How's that sound?"

"That sounds awesome, Clay! All except the dead horse part," he confessed.

With Rennie in the room I decided to text Maggie rather than call her. I wished that I could be with her, and to finally be able to confess my secret life as an avenging vigilante. Next week seemed like a long time off, and yet how she might react to the truth was something I didn't mind delaying, either. Secrets! Hell! Killing people!

Chapter 10

MISTER WALLACE BANE and Doctor Mortimer Chestnut were about as different as night and day, and yet both of them had become fixated on Clay Arnold's visit to Kissinger College next week.

Wallace walked around the exterior of the Von Timm Observatory inspecting the work that he and Clarabelle had completed in the last couple of days. It was looking very good, and he figured that with her help, everything would be in tip-top shape as Dr. Chestnut had demanded. He walked inside the observatory's entrance hall and took inventory of the work he still needed to complete.

"Not too bad. Some fresh paint, wash the windows, polish the floors, replace lightbulbs, clean the bathroom. All manageable, especially with Ms. Meemo's help. And what's that all about? Why is she being so nice to me? I do appreciate her help . . . and her company, but I really need to stay focused on that Clay Arnold astro-wannabe. Honorary doctorate, my eye! Everyone gets to be called doctor but me! And that pretty girlfriend of his, Maggie Bodine. Aaarrggghh," he moaned, and his mood darkened. "I better go below and straighten up my office and prepare the blocked-off storage space for, uh, company."

Wallace the Mole worked out of his subterranean office beneath the Vonn Timm Observatory his entire career. He spent more waking hours here than he did at his own home in town. In fact, he rarely went home, so this was essentially where he lived. And if anyone else ever ventured down here, which was indeed infrequently, they never stayed too long.

In the main, Wallace was happy here. He was often left alone because his colleagues essentially ignored him unless they needed his help. But he was mainly happy because when everyone else had left campus for the day, he could take as much time as he wanted pointing the Clark telescope to some obscure nebula or star cluster. Over the years he had become a very competent astronomer, and his astrophotography had improved significantly. Good enough to earn him an honorable mention by *Space and Beyond* magazine.

Wallace whispered to himself, "I need to determine the very best time and place to kidnap Ms. Bodine and keep her hidden away to prove to Dr. Clay Arnold that unpleasant things can happen to people who live charmed existences. Yes, indeed! And of course, I would never hurt her. I just want to prove that I can outdo the ones who get all of the credit."

Wallace caught a glimpse of his face in the mirror above his sink. "How pathetic I look," he whimpered. But that only strengthened his resolve to prove himself . . . if only to himself. Wallace leaned heavily against the side of his tall bookcase, and with some effort he was able to move it enough to reveal a hidden door. He opened the door, flipped a light switch and peered into the eight-by-ten foot storage room beyond. He spent the next hour clearing out office flotsam that had languished there for years. Old text books, long-forgotten files, an ancient typewriter, stuff no one cared about. When he was finished, all that remained was a small cot, a single ceiling light, a sink, and a drain in the floor. Then, he took a heavy hammer and drove several metal steeples into the stone walls and attached iron chains to them.

"That should do the trick," he said with satisfaction. "Now I need to pay a visit to our science lab and see if I can borrow some ether. I'll tell them it's to help clean the telescope's optics. Then, we should be all set."

Wallace turned off the light in the storage room, closed its soundproof door, and repositioned the bookcase in front of the door. He caught another glimpse of himself in his mirror and stared back at his reflection for a long time. "I'm sorry, but this is something that I really need to do . . . ."

———

Meanwhile, seated in his office in the Kurtzmann Science Center, Dr. Mortimer Chestnut stared intently at his office computer screen. He was attempting to craft his own kidnap plan. He even titled it "Operation Perseus". So far, his plan was to kidnap Maggie Bodine after the ceremony for Clay Arnold and transport her to his cabin hidden in the woods off County Road 250 North. He knew his plan needed work, but he was determined to come across as a hero in front of President Murray and the college's board of trustees. Like mythological Perseus saving chained princess Andromeda from the sea monster, Mortimer planned to swoop in, free the kidnapped Ms. Bodine, and save the day.

"Well, at least I have the cabin ready for its 'guest'. Now I need to try to consider all eventualities and devise a plan that implicates the most vulnerable among us, the lowest of the low, Mr. Wallace Bane." Mortimer smiled at his nasty cleverness.

A few moments later Mortimer was roused from his reverie by a knock on his office door.

"Yes," he called out. "What is it?"

Ms. Meemo appeared in his doorway. "I'll be leaving soon, Dr. Chestnut. Is there anything you require before I go?"

"No, Ms. Meemo," he replied. "I think I have everything very well in hand. Please contact Mr. Bane in the morning to assure that he is fulfilling his responsibilities for the reception at the observatory next week. We certainly wouldn't want anything to go awry, now would we? Remember, we want everything to be tip-top." He shot her one of his frosty smiles.

Ms. Meemo couldn't exit their office suite fast enough. "That man just gives me the creeps!" she said out loud. "He's never in a good mood. I wonder what he's up to."

Chapter 11

After our naps Rennie and I both felt refreshed and eager to see what we could in and around the town of Moab. We drove down the main street and still saw a good number of tourists visiting trendy shops and restaurants even though most folks had their school-age children back home already.

"Look at that!" Rennie yelped, and he pointed at an amazing wooden cigar store Indian on silent duty at the entrance to a rock and mineral shop. Everywhere Rennie turned he saw things that he never knew existed . . . fossils, large amethyst minerals, bronze sculptures of cowboys, dead rattlesnakes, old firearms, gold coins, miner's lamps, and on and

on. I had a feeling this would be a trip that Rennie would remember for a very long time, and I was delighted to be part of it.

"How about we sit outside at this Mexican restaurant, Rennie? That way we can check out the people and cars as they go by.

"I'm game. Tori has been teaching me a little Spanish. I don't know much, but maybe I could try it a little. Think that would be okay, Clay?"

"Sure, why not, *mi amigo?!*

We had a great meal, and Rennie did in fact get to practice his Spanish *"un poco"* with our waitress, Aurora, who was good-natured and helped him pronounce his words a little better.

"Buenos dias, Aurora!" Rennie said to our waitress as we were leaving.

"Noches, Senor Rennie," our waitress said. *"Buenos Noches.* It's evening now, my friend."

We took our time walking back to where we parked our car. The sun was already behind the mountains, and with each minute that passed the night sky grew darker and the town lights came on. We climbed back into the Lexus and headed north through town. We traversed the Colorado River, and in just a couple of minutes we were back on highway 191 with the rocky landscape looming over us. We passed the entrance for Arches National Park which was closed due to road repairs, and after driving another ten minutes, we turned west at a road sign pointing to Canyonlands National Park and our destination, Dead Horse Point.

"Oh man, what's that?!" Rennie squealed. Sure enough there was a dead cow in the prairie grass about twenty feet from the road. It was laying on its side but its legs were sticking straight out as stiff as boards.

"You said we wouldn't see any dead horses, but you never said anything about dead cows!" Rennie laughed. "Can we get out and look at it?"

I couldn't help but smile to myself about how typical it was for a kid Rennie's age to want to see, smell, and touch a dead cow "Why don't we just keep going, Rennie? I promise you we'll see really cool stuff at the end of the road."

By the time we got to the end of the road, the sun was nearly below the mountains, and most of the park's visitors had already returned to their cars. The last dying rays of sunlight lit up the canyon walls that contained the Colorado River. The gold, orange, and red colors of the rocks put on a magical spectacle for us, and when they faded to black in the darkness of night, the stars came out.

"Okay," I said. "Let's go over a few important points before we get started. First, we're basically standing on a huge cliff, and it is a very long way down to the bottom. So rule number one: No running. There are no guard rails here. Second: We stick together. We both have our headlamps, but it can be easy to get confused where you are in the dark. Third: Respect the land. We'll leave no trace behind that we've been here, okay? And Fourth: Protect our gear. We've traveled a long way for this job, and we need to make sure we protect what pays our salary. *Comprende?!"*

"Si, yo comprendo todo, Senor Clay," Rennie replied.

We both positioned our cameras on tripods next to each other and waited a few minutes longer for the night sky to get even darker. We faced south so that we could get the full benefit of the galactic core of the Milky Way.

"Focusing in the dark is always a challenge, so let me show you where to set your focusing ring. Now set your shutter speed for twenty-five seconds, your aperture at f/2.8, your ISO at 1600, and the white balance at 5,000 Kelvin."

Rennie did exactly as I instructed and was rewarded with his very first-ever scene of the Milky Way. "Oh man, Clay, look at all of those stars! My camera sees way more than my eyes do!"

"Welcome to the universe, my friend! Now you know why I suggested to Chris Hazeltine that we include some images of the night sky for his promotional work."

We both took several more pictures from our vantage point one thousand feet above the Colorado River. Nearly everyone was gone from the park now, but we heard young children running and squealing with delight under the grandeur of the stars.

"Rennie, I'm going back to the Lexus and get our intervalometers so we can make some very long exposures to create star trails," I said. "You stay here, and I'll be back in a sec."

I walked back toward the parking lot and was fascinated by the gnarled shapes of the Bristlecone Pines. I stopped to take a few pictures and then headed on toward our car. The night was quiet with the exception of the children's voices, and everything seemed perfect. Then it happened. I heard a little girl's voice suddenly break into a shriek of fear, and I had a feeling she had ventured too close to the cliff edge. I immediately took off for where I left Rennie, but when I got there, he was nowhere to be seen. I heard another cry of fear about twenty feet away, and went in that direction.

"Rennie, where are you?" I called out. At first there was no reply. "Rennie!" I called again.

"We're down here, Clay," came his muffled voice.

I carefully walked to the cliff's edge, and with my head lamp on, I peered into the abyss. The only thing I could think of was that it was one thousand feet to the canyon floor below. I called out to Rennie again, and his voice helped me locate exactly where he was.

"Oh no!" I said as I saw both him and a little girl clinging to the most fragile of bushes with nothing between them and sure death but air. Rennie had heard the little girl slide over the edge and ran to help her. He had carefully slid down about ten feet to where she was hanging on for dear life and managed to wrap one arm around her tightly while he clung to a Bristlecone root.

"I've got her, Clay, but I don't know how much longer we can hang on," Rennie said with remarkable composure.

A moment later the girl's father appeared with a frantic look in his eyes. "I've got a rope, but I'm not sure it's long enough," he said with more fear rising in his voice.

I grabbed the rope, tied it around my waist, and gingerly crawled over the cliff edge. I hung on to an outcrop of rock and let the rope dangle downward and hollered to Rennie to feel for it.

"I got it, Clay, but I don't think you'll be able to pull us both up. I'm tying the rope around the girl. Pull her up first. I think I'll be okay, but hurry!"

I did as he instructed, and two minutes later, I had the terrified girl in my arms and was able to safely pass her up to her father.

"She's safe, Rennie, now let's get you up here."
No sooner had I said that when I heard the sound of
crumbling sandstone. I looked down and saw that
Rennie had slid down the cliff face another six feet
and was hanging on to a tree root that looked like
it could be yanked free at any moment.

"I'm coming, Rennie, just hang on!" I managed
to tie the rope to a stout bush and slowly lowered
myself down to where he and the girl were first,
and then I retied the rope so I could drop another
six feet to where Rennie Cotton was hanging on for
dear life. As soon as I arrived, Rennie wrapped his
legs around my waist and clung on as I managed to
pull us up a few feet. By then, the girl's father was
able to find a longer rope and threw it over the cliff
face to us. With some effort, we were finally able to
drag our scratched and bruised bodies to the top
of the escarpment gasping for breath. We both lay
there for a few moments staring up at the stars and
thinking about how lucky we were.

The girl's father stood over us with tears in his
eyes. "I can't thank you enough," came his sob-
filled voice. "Young man," he said to Rennie, "that
was about the bravest thing I ever saw anyone do.
Thank you for saving my little girl."

Rennie and I managed to regain our footing,
and the little girl's father brought his daughter to

where we were. She ran to Rennie and hugged him as tightly as she could. The father and I made eye contact, and it was clear we were thinking the same thing, that things would've turned out disastrously had it not been for Rennie's fast action. Rennie and I both agreed that we'd had more than enough excitement for one night and walked over to collect our camera gear. We rejoined the young family in the parking lot, and shared some water while we got better acquainted.

"I'm Rennie," he said to the little girl. "I don't think we had a chance to be properly introduced down there," he quipped. She smiled at him and gave him another hug. "You're my hero, Rennie," she cried. "You're both our heroes," the girl's father declared, and after a few minutes of regaining our emotional equilibrium, we exchanged contact information and went our separate ways.

Rennie and I got in the Lexus, and he turned to me. "I get it, Clay," he said.

"Get what?" I asked.

"Rules number one and two: No running, and we stick together!"

I squeezed his shoulder in acknowledgment, and we headed back toward Moab. On the way we saw the dead cow again, but this time Rennie had no interest in checking out death up close and personal.

The course of the next two days went much more smoothly for us. We took plenty of daytime images at Arches National Park and Canyonlands. We saved our last night for driving west a couple of hours to Goblin Valley State Park and shooting pictures of the sandstone hoodoos beneath the Milky Way. We met with Chris Hazeltine the next morning at the motel, and he was very pleased with several of the pictures we showed him.

"Chris, when I get back home, these pics will become even more dramatic once I've had a chance to work on them in Lightroom and Photoshop."

"I'm really happy with what I'm seeing already, Clay. You and Rennie have done a great job for our visitors association, and we'll be happy to give Rennie proper photo credit. Just let me know when you're ready to talk more."

That made my young associate very happy. Me, too.

We left later that day for the drive back to Salt Lake City. This time we chose not to stop in the town of Price. It was remarkable to me just how much closer Rennie and I became in just a few short days. We drove long stretches without saying much. He spent time fiddling with his camera and looking through the manual. He was hooked on photography and asked me questions from time to time. Otherwise, we were just two guys on the road whose friendship had been made even stronger. We had been to the precipice of mortality and came away knowing just how sacred and fragile life can be, and how important the bonds of friendship are. Facing death together will do that to you.

Chapter 12

W E ARRIVED HOME AT the brewery complex late the next afternoon and were really glad to be back home. In the main the trip had been a good one, but being back home with Tori, Weed, Mace, Lex, and Satchmo was even better. As I thought about it, I became more aware of my owning shifting emotions. A year ago I would've killed that biker who assaulted Rennie in Price without batting an eye. Hell, the son of a bitch deserved it. Now, with so much time having passed since Jennifer was murdered in the Planned Parenthood bombing, and with my desire to be fully transparent with Maggie, I found the beast inside me subsiding.

But I have to admit that I have a violent history, and I doubt whether its fully run its course.

I joined the others at the farmhouse for dinner. Tori and Weed brought us up to speed on how their rehearsing was going for their musical gig at Stella's Diner this weekend. Mace, in his inimitable way, quietly listened to his friends with Lex at his feet. And, of course, everyone wanted to hear about Rennie's and my adventure to Utah.

"Why don't you tell them about our trip, Rennie?" I urged. I was curious to see what he would tell and what he'd hold back. Not surprisingly, he shared a lot about the positive aspects of our trip: The travel, the scenery, learning the basics about his camera and earning photo credit for his images, flying in planes, speaking Spanish, and, of course, the dead cow.

"Should I tell them about the other stuff, too, Clay?" he asked.

"What other stuff?" Tori asked with real concern.

"It's your choice," I said to Rennie.

Rennie went over and sat on the arm of Mace's chair and leaned against his older friend. He began to relate the less positive things that had occurred, too, including the biker redneck in Price, and how I fried his Harley. Then, he told the story about the near-death experience for him and the little girl at Dead Horse Point.

Tori gasped in shock, and Weed about choked on his harmonica. Mace sat there stoically listening, and a broad smile crossed his face when Rennie talked about helping the little girl. He gave me credit, too. I guess the part of his stories that I appreciated the most was how he actually expressed himself. Before the trip, he might've told these accounts with youthful exuberance and some exaggeration. Tonight he described what happened matter-of-factly, with a more adult demeanor. I was proud of him.

"Clay Arnold, I swear . . ." Tori chided. "And you said you'd keep an eye on him!"

I was about to speak when Rennie came to my defense. "Clay saved my butt twice, Tori, so please don't go giving him a rough time. He's the real hero."

Tori relented and all of us got comfortable on the porch listening to music and hearing each others' stories about things big and small. Around nine thirty, I announced it was time for me to hit the sack, and Satchmo and I ambled across the courtyard to my place.

I spent the remainder of the evening alone. Well, me and Satchmo that is. I needed to put my camera equipment away, do some laundry, and upload the images from our Utah trip in my computer. I also just wanted to do some thinking before I called Maggie. About ten thirty I picked up the phone and called her.

"There you are!" she said brightly. "I was wondering when I would hear your rakish voice again," she teased.

"Hi, sweetheart, it's great to hear your voice, too. I sure wanted to talk with you when Rennie and I were in Utah, but it wasn't always opportune. I'm sorry I only texted you."

"Not a problem, Clay. Besides we're going to be together in two days. I can't wait to see you, and I know that Laura is really excited about our trip. How was your time around Moab? Did Rennie enjoy his first real travel experience?"

"Our trip was very good. Chris Hazeltine has been easy to work with, and you might consider contacting him at some point for some of your promotional consulting. We did have a couple of episodes, but like Shakespeare wrote, 'all's well that ends well.'"

"Oh!" Maggie said with a tinge of concern in her voice. "What do you mean by 'episodes'?"

I decided to put off telling her about how I handled the biker in Price until the end. So I told her about what happened at Dead Horse Point. The timbre of her voice fell and rose with concern, relief, and then pride when I told her about how Rennie had saved the little girl's life.

"Omigod! You're kidding me! That is amazing. What a great kid! I can't wait for Laura to meet him."

"He was a hero," I stated. "Plus, we traveled together very well. And now I get to see you! Life's good."

"Alright, Clay, you used the plural a moment ago when you mentioned 'episodes'. What else happened that you're not telling me?"

"Well," I slowly began. "It was like this. We spent the first night at a motel in Price, Utah, and this rather large brutish biker starting giving Rennie a rough time at the pool because he's black. I wasn't there, but I believe Rennie when he said he didn't doing anything out of line. So, the next morning when we were checking out and loading our car, this same guy grabs Rennie in the parking lot and was about to really hurt him when I stepped in."

"And then?" Maggie asked.

"Maggie, I swear I did my best to defuse the situation, but this guy was big and behaving very aggressively. He wasn't interested in being reasonable, so I helped him attain situational enlightenment!"

"Oh, and what does that mean?" she prodded.

"Sometimes when I'm traveling with expensive equipment, I carry a stun gun of sorts with me just in case."

"And?" Maggie prompted.

"Well, I gave him a choice, either him or his bike. I actually recall flashing on you and wondering what you'd want me to do. Anyway, I picked his Harley and used the stun gun to fry all of the bike's electrical wiring."

"You're kidding me. You ruined that guy's motorcycle?"

"Yeah, pretty much," I said. "But the good news is I didn't kill him, and honestly Maggie, given what he was preparing to do to Rennie, I really did want to kill him."

Those words hung in the air for what seemed like a very long several seconds.

"Whoa!" Maggie exhaled. "That was an 'episode'. I don't think I've ever heard you speak so violently before, Clay. I mean, I understand why you would be angry under the circumstances, but thinking about killing the guy and ruining his motorcycle . . . that's pretty tough stuff."

I knew that the door was now open for me to come clean about my being a vigilante. She needs to know that I am someone who believes in evening the score for the good guys. I hesitated briefly and then leaped through the door.

"Maggie, this was actually what I wanted to discuss with you in person, and there's more that I need to share with you, but I don't think doing it over the phone is fair to either of us. We can talk when you and Laura come, okay?"

There was momentary silence on her end, so I repeated the same question. Her reply was somewhat distant, and I felt my heart beginning to sink for fear that she had changed her mind about coming to be with me. "Can we please talk more about this when you're here?" I implored.

"Yes," came her terse reply. "Look, Clay, I have to go now. We'll talk when I'm there."

"I love you very much, Maggie, and can't wait to be with you," I said.

"I love you, too, Clay. See you in two days. Goodnight." Then she hung up, and I was alone with my big cat and a head filled with worry.

Thankfully the next day and a half were very busy for me. I had been contacted by President Murray's office to confirm details for our visit to Kissinger College in Greencastle. I also had a bunch of work that I needed to do with my Utah images while the experience was still fresh in my mind. And, of course, there were a ton of things that Tori, Weed, Mace, Rennie, and I wanted to do around the brewery complex to make it neat and comfortable for Laura and Maggie.

I replayed my last conversation with Maggie over in my mind repeatedly, and no matter how I tried to put a positive spin on it, I always ended with the same results. For the first time in our relationship, there were serious, unsettling doubts.

"Fasten your seat belts, everyone! We may be in for a bumpy ride!"

Chapter 13

RENNIE AND I CRUISED along I-70 West in my Tacoma and took the exit for the Indianapolis airport. A mile or so later we took the exit for the cell phone lot and found a space for the truck. We pulled in and parked to await their phone call.

"So what's she like?" Rennie asked.

"What's who like?" I replied. "Maggie or Laura?

"Both!" Rennie said. "I don't know either of them. All I know is that you get all mushy-like when you talk about Maggie," he laughed.

"Yeah, well, wait till you meet Maggie, and you'll understand why," I said. "As for Laura, I've never met her, either, or her parents, but if she looks

anything like Maggie, we'll have a plethora of pulchritude around us for the next few days."

"Say what?! What's a pleth of pulcher?" Rennie asked.

"You know, really pretty girls!" I replied. "All I can tell you about Laura is that she's Maggie's sister's daughter, and she's fourteen, and supposedly really smart. So, she's just a little older than you are, Rennie. I hope you guys get along well."

"Me, too," he said. "I promise to be nice to her. I hope she's not too smart."

We sat in the car for a while longer. Rennie occupied himself with his camera, and I occupied myself by fretting over how Maggie was going to react when she saw me. There were more than a few times over the last two days that I regretted telling her about my evening the score with the biker in Price, and now she knows there's even more information to follow. I closed my eyes and shook my head in disbelief that I had said anything at all to Maggie. And yet, how could I not tell her. First and foremost, it's who I am and what I've done. That doesn't mean that I'm going to live the rest of my life as an avenging vigilante. Honestly, my blood doesn't boil like it used to when I felt provoked. I give Maggie's positive influence on me a lot of credit for that. On the other hand, I have witnessed far too many transgressions foisted upon innocent victims to stand idly by without reacting. Hopefully, Maggie and I can come to an understanding about that. I really do love her, but I can't change the way I'm wired, either. Can I?

A few moments later my cell phone rang, and Maggie told me that they'd landed, gotten their luggage, and were waiting outside of the baggage claim area. We took off for the terminal. I was really excited to see her and scared shitless at the same time. I saw Maggie and Laura standing by the curb. We pulled over and got out.

She was a vision! To me, Maggie Bodine is the prettiest girl on the planet, and seeing her smiling face with her auburn hair backlit by the late afternoon sun, she was indeed a vision. We fell into each other's arms in a consuming hug. I didn't want to let go, but I knew Rennie and Laura were waiting in the wings.

"Back to you in a minute!" I growled lustily to Maggie as we both took care of making introductions all around while also piling luggage into the bed of the Tacoma. Maggie joined me in the front seat and Laura and Rennie were in the backseat.

Maggie leaned against me briefly and rested her head on my shoulder. That was enough reassurance for me for now.

I looked at Laura in the rearview mirror and said, "Laura, we are so thrilled that you're here with us, aren't we, Rennie?"

Rennie nodded his agreement and looked over at Laura really for the first time. "Yeah, we've all been talking about you a lot. Lex and Satchmo and I have all sorts of things we want to show you at home."

Laura wasn't exactly sure who Lex and Satchmo were, but she smiled and nodded affirmatively. I looked over at Maggie's pretty face and damn near melted. "God, I've missed you!" I whispered.

"Me, too. How long until we get to your place?"

"Thirty long minutes," I smiled.

The ride home to the brewery complex was filled with the cacophonous sound of cross chatter, with questions and answers flying in all directions. I was delighted to see that everyone was getting along.

"Clay and I saw a dead cow in Utah," Rennie announced. "Its legs were sticking straight out."

Not exactly sure what to say, Laura offered the most positive reply she could think of, "Lovely. Cows are nice. I like cows . . . preferably live ones."

Almost exactly thirty minutes later we pulled into our driveway and came to a stop in the courtyard. I was surprised by how nice everything looked. After Rennie and I had left for the airport, Weed, Tori, and, Mace rushed outside to put up a banner across the entrance to our home welcoming Laura and Maggie. There were twinkle lights strung everywhere and a dozen potted mums situated all around the courtyard giving the brewery complex a festive fall look. I was very touched that my friends went to such thoughtful efforts to help make Maggie and her niece feel so welcome.

"Well this is it!" I said moving my arms in a sweeping motion, and with that Tori, Weed, Mace, Lex, and Satchmo came striding out of the farmhouse to greet our guests.

"You guys are incredible!" I shouted at them.

I don't know to describe it any better than to say there was a whole lot of smiling and hugging going on.

"I swear I feel like I already know each of you because Clay talks about you all the time," Maggie said. "It's just wonderful putting faces with names. Thank you so much for welcoming Laura and me here."

"We're thrilled you're finally here," Tori said, and she stepped closer to Maggie and Laura. "Do you mind if I touch your faces? I want to feel what you look like."

Both Laura and Maggie were very touched by Tori's unique way of getting to know one another. "Of course," Maggie replied. Laura followed, and when Tori touched her face, Laura gently extended her hands and touched Tori's face as well. It was a very tender connection between three human beings, and I think each of us watching was drawn in by the beauty of the moment. I had no doubt that the three of them could become fast friends.

And, of course, Mace and Weed got into the act and added their welcomes with playful promises of telling inappropriate stories about that rascal, Clay Arnold. They suggested that they might have to imbibe in some Four Roses bourbon first to lubricate their memories. I feigned a heart attack.

"Wow, you really do live in an old beer brewery complex!" Laura exclaimed as she looked at our buildings surrounding the courtyard."

"Yeah!" Rennie said. "Why don't you put your stuff away, and Lex and I'll give you the grand tour."

"Give us thirty minutes, Rennie," I suggested. "I want to get them settled in my place and maybe give them a little tour of the camera museum, too. Then you and Laura can go off exploring as much as you want. How's that sound, guys?"

Both Rennie and Laura nodded their agreement, and Maggie, Laura, and I grabbed the luggage and headed for my place. And, of course, Satchmo led the way.

"They're terrific!" Maggie said and nodded in the direction where Mace, Tori, and Weed were standing.

I hugged her as we walked and said, "Thanks, Maggie. They're my family. All of them."

We entered my brew house abode and took the elevator to the main level. I enjoyed watching Laura and Maggie's reaction as we entered my living space. The combination of my photos on the walls, contemporary furniture and lighting, hardwood floors, and woven carpets made for a comfortable and chic environment. I could tell that Maggie liked what she saw. I showed Laura to the guest room and showed her how to use the toggle switches to control her lights and window blinds, and how to operate the water jets in the Jacuzzi.

"Laura, why don't you change your clothes into something more casual, and I'll show Maggie our room. Then, I'll make us a quick snack before you join Rennie. Okay with you?"

"Sounds perf!" she replied.

Maggie and I walked up the open staircase to my spacious bedroom and she smiled as she looked around and saw my antique brass bed surrounded by more contemporary furniture and even more of my photography positioned next to some of the rarest early Daguerreotype cameras in the world. The prize pieces in my collection.

"Wow, Clay, I had no idea," she said softly, but that was about as far as she got verbally as I pulled her close to me, and we kissed and held each other as two lovers do when they've been apart for a while.

"Now this is what I call a snack!" I said breathlessly.

"Easy, big fella, we have a young one down-stairs, and you've promised her something to eat. Then, if you make a really good snack," she teased, "I may let you have your sweet way with me!"

"You got a deal!"

We rejoined Laura downstairs in the kitchen, and we basically grazed on some of the healthy goodies I had purchased . . . fruit, nuts, peanut butter on zucchini bread, yogurt. Obviously I was trying to stay in Maggie's good graces.

"And please don't think you need to ask my permission to raid the refrigerator," I said. "Whatever you find is fair game."

"Be careful what you offer, kind sir," came Maggie's cautionary reply.

"I'll second that!" Laura added. "This is just great, Clay, thank you. So, how do I find Rennie now?"

"I'll text him. You take the elevator down one level to the courtyard, and I bet he'll be waiting for you. Have a great time!"

Maggie added, "There's no timetable, Laura. Have fun. Just be back in time to clean up for our dinner with Tori, Weed, and Mace, okay?"

A moment later Laura was out the door to see all the neat stuff around the brewery complex that Rennie was going to show her.

"So, how'd you enjoy your snack?" I asked with playful curiosity. "Do you think that it qualified as, uh, what was your expression? Oh yeah, 'really good'?"

"Perhaps," she said as she walked out of the kitchen and headed for the stairway leading to the bedroom. She stopped midway up the stairs and turned to look at me. She smiled and said, "Coming?"

Well, let's just say that I didn't need to be asked twice. When I got to the bedroom, Maggie had gone into the bathroom. She briefly poked her head out and said, "Practice patience!"

"Swell," I said under my breath. I took my time disrobing and ditched my briefs as I slid under the covers. I turned down the lights and lit a candle and turned on an instrumental folk music station. Then my patience was rewarded when Maggie came out wearing a lavender satin night shirt and a smile. Her auburn hair looked the color of a dark reddish honey and her skin glowed in the candlelight. She was indeed a vision.

Maggie slid in to bed and formed her body next to mine. The smell of her skin and flashes of color from her green eyes were altogether alluring and mesmerizing. There was absolutely no place on the planet that I would rather be.

We kissed and held for an incredible several minutes, arms and legs winding and wrapping and repeating. We even talked a little.

"I can't believe you're really here, Maggie. I am so glad you and Laura could come."

"Me, too, Clay," she said softly. "I've really missed you a lot, more than you probably know, and with your getting the honorary degree, well, this is where I should be, Dr. Arnold."

Her words really touched me, and I felt more confident to ask if we needed to talk about my Price biker experience anymore right now. "I just feel a need to clear the air with you, and I'm honestly really concerned that I frightened you on the phone last time."

"I was and am concerned, especially since you say there's more you want to tell me. I do have questions, but I don't want to talk about it right now, Clay. Right now I just want us to get back to being us. So, if you don't mind, Dr. Arnold, can we talk about this a little later?"

And with those words she pulled me close, and all of our cares drifted, wafted, melted, and dissolved as we became one.

Chapter 14

A COUPLE OF HOURS LATER Laura came running into my home with Rennie and Lex in hot pursuit. They'd been all over the brewery complex, and they weren't finished exploring yet. They were out of breath from laughing and carrying on.

"I haven't even shown you Clay's photo lab yet!" Rennie said.

Maggie and I had indeed gotten back to us being us, and we were now fully clothed and hanging out on my roof garden.

"Hey, we're up here," I hollered down to the kids. "C'mon up!"

Despite having only three legs, Lex led the charge up the steps, and Laura and Rennie joined us as we looked over our property and the White River as it silently flowed past the walnut grove several yards away.

"And what have you two been up to?" Maggie asked.

"You won't believe this place, Aunt Maggie, it's incredible!" Laura lauded. "Rennie showed me the farmhouse, and Tori gave me a tour of the garden. Tonight's dinner will include some kale and tomatoes and peppers and garlic, all that she and Rennie grew. Then Rennie showed me the power plant where he and Mace live, and Mace told me some of the history of the complex when it was a woodworking mill and the old beer brewery before that."

Rennie chimed in, "I even showed Laura where Mace zapped that mean Clement Hacker on the farmhouse porch. Just fried that redneck before he could kill Clay and Tori."

Maggie's eyebrows shot up in surprise.

"Uh, I told you about that, right?" I said to Maggie quizzically.

"Yes you did, Clay, I just didn't know that Laura was going to get, uh, full disclosure about that." She gently bonked Rennie on top of his head with her fist for being so forthcoming.

"Okay guys, it's seven o'clock now," I said. "Tori wants us at the farmhouse at seven thirty, so why don't we all go get cleaned up and then hook up again for dinner?"

And that's what we did.

Laura, Maggie, and I strolled across the courtyard and were greeted by Weed who sat on a porch chair with his feet propped up on a hand rail. He had a glass of Four Roses by his elbow and a smile on his face. He was coaxing the mournful sounds of an old blues tune from his harmonica.

"Hi there, everyone!" he said as we joined him on the porch. The sun was starting to get low in the sky and its last streaks of orange and red backlit his frame like a stage show.

"And howdy to you, too, Mr. Weed," came Laura's amicable reply.

"Uh, no mister, just Weed," he replied and then he blew a long blues riff just to show off a little for his audience.

A few moments later Mace and Lex sashayed from the power plant to the porch. Laura saw the three-legged black Lab limping and said to Rennie, "I don't think I asked you how he lost his leg earlier."

"Aw, he got shot last year by that mean Hacker man when Lex tried to keep his brother from hurting Tori on the path by the river."

Again, Maggie's eyebrows went up in surprise. "I don't think you told me about that, Clay."

"Well, it wasn't a pleasant experience, and it happened before we met again, so I guess I just sorta forgot," I fibbed.

Maggie looked at Clay and said, "Really, you just sorta forgot Tori getting attacked and your dog getting shot?"

I shrugged sheepishly, and Mace saved my ass by changing the subject.

"Laura, I'm sure we'd all love to hear about your life in Santa Fe. Whatever you feel like sharing."

"Well, I dunno," she began. "I pretty much go to school and hang out with my friends."

"Why don't you tell them about your artwork?" Maggie encouraged.

"I guess I paint a little," she confessed. "I like Georgia O'Keeffe's paintings and Frida Kahlo, too. I don't try to copy their art, but I do feel inspired by their work. I especially like how Georgia O'Keeffe used bright light on her subjects."

The mention of light got my attention, and I made a mental note to talk with her some more about it.

Tori called to us from inside and said that dinner was almost ready, but that she could use a little help setting the table, etc. Rennie and Laura immediately got up to lend a hand, and I went in to help, too, leaving Maggie with Mace and Weed on the porch. I thought it was a good way for

Maggie to get to know my friends better without my presence.

"So, you two fellas know Clay about as well as anyone," Maggie said.

"Only since we were about four years old," Weed replied. "Me and Tori both. We lived down the road a little, and Tori and I went all the way through school with Clay. Yeah, I'd say we know him pretty well."

"He's been awfully good to me," Mace stated. "When he bought this place, the deal with the owner, Mr. Jeffries, was that I could live the remainder of my days here if I chose to. At that time there was no way that either of us would know that we'd become as close as we are. All of us really, and we're even closer when anyone of us is threatened by outside forces."

"You mean like last year with the Hacker men?" Maggie asked.

"For sure!" Weed added. "None of us went looking for conflict, but I'm sure we were all glad that we had each other's backs when it happened."

"I hope you guys know how much I love Clay, but the violence is something that frightens me," Maggie confessed. "It also makes me wonder how well I really know Clay."

Weed and Mace looked at each other and were thinking the same thing: If only Maggie really knew how much of an avenging vigilante Clay has been. But the two men chose not to say anything further. Both men learned a long time ago that love relationships can change, and sometimes it's better to keep your cards close to your vest. In this case they didn't want to risk Maggie getting upset with Clay at some point and reporting him to the authorities. And if the truth be known, they knew they were complicit to Clay's violence by helping to construct his clandestine weapons. No, better to let Clay and Maggie have this conversation on their own.

"I will tell you this, Maggie," Weed said. "The Clay Arnold you know is about as fine a man as there is." Weed scanned the brewery complex with his arms. "None of this and none of us would be the family we are if it weren't for Clay. We stand by him 100 percent because he's been there for each of us . . . and that includes you, too, Maggie. There's nothing he wouldn't do for you."

Their conversation was cut short by Tori's call for them to come to the table, but the three of them took a final moment to talk.

"I would simply ask you to remember one thing, Maggie," Mace said. "None of us is perfect, but our friend, Clay Arnold, is the real deal. You can rest assured that your emotional investment in him is worth it and that any risk you perceive is definitely worth the reward."

Maggie nodded her understanding, but both Mace and Weed knew she would need to experience more of Clay's nature before she understood his true value as they did. They went inside to join the others already seated at the table.

"Okay y'all," Tori began. "Now before we dive in, I just want to say how delighted we are that Maggie and Laura are with us, and that we hope you return as often as you can. You're part of us now. And congratulations to Mr. Rennie Cotton for helping save that girl in Utah. Also want to say how very proud we are of Clay for his receiving an honorary doctorate tomorrow. Very cool, and it couldn't happen to a more deserving man. So guys, how about a toast to Laura, Maggie, Rennie, and Clay? Oh heck, let's just make it a toast to all of us!"

Everyone got into the spirit, including Lex and Satchmo, and I had a premonition that my brewery family was going to get larger in the not-too-distant future. It was a good feeling. I looked around the table at each face and felt a sense of deep devotion. When I looked at Maggie, she smiled back at me, and I knew how much I wanted her to be happy. We leaned into each other, and I playfully whispered, "Is it snack time yet?"

We partied well past midnight and into a new day.

Chapter 15

For Wallace Bane the day he'd long been waiting for had finally arrived. Today he'd see his astrophotography nemesis, Clay Arnold, and teach that man a lesson. For the umpteenth time, Wallace the Mole surveyed the grounds outside of the Von Timm Observatory to make sure everything was in readiness for the honorary doctorate ceremony and the reception scheduled to follow. The perimeter looked immaculate, and the white domed observatory shone like a celestial jewel.

The interior of the observatory was equally as spotless. The walls had been painted, the floors and windows washed, and the bathrooms cleaned

like a surgical suite. And the Clark telescope was calibrated and the lenses cleaned for perfect viewing. In Wallace's office in the basement, everything was neat and tidy, and the hidden storeroom was ready for its "guest". Everything was in readiness.

"Had it not been for Clarabelle Meemo, I doubt I could have pulled it off. I never would've had the kind of influence with the Facilities Management staff that she did, plus she just seemed to have a special knack for getting things done. So, Dr. Chestnut, you said you wanted everything to be 'tip-top', well sir, tip-top it is!"

Meanwhile across campus, Dr. Mortimer Chestnut hummed to himself with his eyes fixated on his computer monitor. He was intent on making certain that everything was prepared for the day's festivities at the Von Timm Observatory and his much-deserved vacation.

"Ms. Meemo, I want you to go over to the observatory and help Mr. Bane with any last minute details that might come up. With celebrities like Clay Arnold and Dr. Wade Henry coming to campus, I'm sure we'll have guests from all over the country, not to mention several media crews."

"But Dr. Chestnut," Clarabelle began, "I was there just yesterday, and I assure you that Wallace, I mean Mr. Bane, has everything in order . . . sir."

"That may be true, Ms. Meemo, but one can never be too prepared. Besides I have some things I need to do before I depart on vacation, and I prefer not to be disturbed."

Clarabelle was taken aback by that last comment. She couldn't imagine what else he needed to do, but she did as her supervisor directed and left the office to join Mr. Bane.

"Now where was I?" Mortimer Chestnut said to himself after Ms. Meemo departed their office suite. "Ah yes!" he exclaimed giddily as he prepared a file containing several e-mails that he wanted secretly sent to Clay Arnold over the next couple of hours.

"This should help lubricate the machinery of chaos to help cover my tracks later today," he mused out loud. He carefully reviewed a message and touched the send key. The first of a series of e-mails was sent from a private e-mail server he'd had installed by a local computer firm outside of the college's IT department.

"Now, all I have to do is show up for the presentation of the honorary doctorate and wait for my time to act," Mortimer murmured aloud. "How sad . . . President Murray will be totally humiliated and whatever pathetic career Wallace Bane had will become even more so. Alas, collateral damage can be so messy."

Meanwhile sixty miles away at the brewery complex, everyone was preparing for the drive to Greencastle for Clay's big day. Since there were seven of them making the trip, it was decided that Rennie and Laura would ride with Clay and Maggie, and Mace, Tori, and Weed would drive separately.

"How do I look?" Maggie asked Clay as she spun around to model her ensemble. She wore a purple dress that was accented with lavender ostrich feathers on the cuffs of her sleeves. Her long auburn hair was beautifully coiffed and gently flowed over her shoulders.

"I swear you look like Venus from a Botticelli painting," Clay praised. "I may be receiving a great award today, but I'm sure all eyes will be on you."

"Knock, knock," came Laura's voice as she ascended the stairs to Clay's bedroom. "Can I come in?"

"Of course, you can," Maggie replied. "Let's see how you look."

Laura walked into the bedroom and spun around just like Maggie had done a few moments earlier.

"Wow!" I exclaimed. "You look terrific, Laura. I swear the two of you are the prettiest girls on the planet." Laura blushed and Maggie helped straighten the hemline to Laura's pale yellow dress. Her soft blonde hair cascaded down her back, and with the jewelry that her mother had loaned her, Laura looked several years older than her true age of fourteen. Maggie sang her praise as well.

"Thank you, guys," Laura replied as she spun around again. "I was hoping you'd like. Oh, by the way, Clay, when I was getting ready I heard your computer beep indicating that you'd received a new e-mail."

"Oh, it was probably my agent, Lily, wishing me good luck today in Greencastle."

"I don't think so," Laura said. I wasn't trying to be nosy, but I couldn't help but see the message when I glanced at the computer. It was weird."

"What was weird about it?" I asked.

"Well, first of all there was this image of a mythological-looking warrior holding a sword and the severed head of a woman with snakes for hair. And then there was this evil sounding laughter."

"That's pretty creepy," Maggie said. "Who would send you a message like that, Clay?"

"I don't know," I said. "If we're all done up here, let's go downstairs to my office and check it out."

We entered my office, and I clicked on my e-mail account. Like Laura said there was a picture just as she'd described with taunting laughter and a printed message that read, "Okay, Dr. Clay Arnold, catch me if you think you're smart enough!"

"I have no idea what that means, and I don't have a clue who sent it, except that it's signed The Mole, whoever that is. I'm sure it's nothing."

Despite my dismissing the message so I didn't alarm Maggie and Laura, I thought back to the e-mail I had received yesterday with another similar taunt. I didn't know what this was about, but I had an uncomfortable nagging feeling that this wasn't the last I'd hear from this Mole person. I kept those thoughts to myself.

We went outside to the courtyard, and Mace, Rennie, Tori, and Weed met us by our vehicles.

"Oooh weee!" I said to Rennie when I saw how handsome the kid looked. He wore new black jeans with black hightop gym shoes, a colorfully printed shirt and a trendy looking jacket. "My, my!" I began. "The girls are gonna go wild, and the boys will all be jealous because you look so sharp."

"I know," Rennie agreed. "I do look pretty badass."

"Language!" Tori reminded him. "Let's keep it clean, young sir."

Mace and Weed looked equally dapper, and Tori looked every bit as beautiful as Laura and Maggie.

"I guess I'll have to change that to the three prettiest girls on the planet," I added. "If you guys are all ready, why don't we load up and hit the road for Greencastle? Next stop Kissinger College and the Von Timm Observatory."

Chapter 16

Dr. Wade Henry and his wife, Kayla, stood on the corner of Washington and Indiana streets in downtown Greencastle. It had been a couple of years since Wade had returned to the area of his youth, and looking around the town square, he was swept up by a flood of emotions.

"My parents used to bring me here when I was a boy. We'd shop at various stores that are no longer here." He pointed to where Fleener's drug store used to be, and Prevo's department store, Troyer's women's clothing, and the Chateau movie theater. All long gone now, except for Headley's hardware store which had relocated down the road.

"After Dad and Mrs. Nathan were killed, Judge Nathan would sometimes bring me to town while mom was at work at the college. He became a wonderful mentor, and everyone in town knew and admired him. I learned a lot just watching him interact with other people. So, I'll always have a soft place in my heart for Putnam County and Greencastle. Seeing it now, though, makes me a little wistful. A lot of time has passed since those days."

Kayla looked at Wade and saw a small tear form at the corner of his eye. She squeezed his hand a little tighter, and he smiled at her for her support. "I know it's hard for you to be here given all of the violence that occurred twenty years ago," Kayla sympathized. "A lot of very good things happened here, too though. Plus, your mom is still here living in the house where you grew up on Brick Chapel Road, and your good friends, Quentin and Luella Harp, still live in the judge's old home across from your mom. A lot of good things."

"I know you're right, Kayla. It still feels very surreal being back here, though. The good news is that our return is for a very exciting reason. Clay Arnold is about as famous as a photographer can get, and his night sky photographs are absolutely stunning. I'm sure the judge would be very pleased that the college is conferring an honorary doctorate on him at the observatory that he endowed. For those reasons, and the ones you mentioned, I am happy to be back here. It's very flattering that President Murray invited me to make the presentation to Clay."

A few minutes later, Wade's mother, Cassie, met them at the entrance to the new Bridges restaurant, and they went inside for lunch.

Wade looked at his watch and said, "I really need to keep an eye on the time. You two can stay here longer and visit if you'd like. I promised President Murray that I would arrive early at the observatory to go over final details for the ceremony."

Cassie responded, "The observatory is only three minutes away, and they've got great service here, so just relax, Wade. You'll get there in plenty of time."

"I know, Mom, I just want everything to go smoothly."

"You'll do great, and besides it's a college ceremony. What could possibly go wrong?"

Wade relaxed, and the three of them reminisced. Cassie had retired recently as the Director of Kissinger College's Stanley Center for Ethics. It was a position that the college asked her to assume in order to continue the good work her late husband had performed as the previous director. Now retired and with no children in the immediate vicinity, Cassie traveled to see them and her old friend in Edmonton, Lucien Kindred.

Dr. Kayla Henry followed in her father's footsteps as a cardiovascular surgeon and somehow managed to balance a very demanding medical career and a healthy home life. Prior to their getting married, Kayla and Wade had a fifteen-year, long-distance relationship while they established their careers, but there was never any doubt that they were devoted to each other. Now, their two children, Thaddeus and Cassiopeia, are college age and currently attending classes.

Wade's meteoric career in astronomy had been launched in a very casual way. Years earlier when young Wade and the judge were neighbors, the judge would often invite Wade to join him in the backyard as they peered heavenward through his telescope at the wonders above. And on several occasions the judge brought Wade along for special viewings through the Clark telescope at the Von Timm Observatory.

After Wade and Thaddeus recovered adequately from the terrible shock of Curly Algol murdering Wade's dad and Thaddeus's wife, they embarked on an oddysey of sorts, driving from the cornfields of Indiana to the majestic clear skies of Alberta, Canada. The trip to Canada was a high school graduation gift from the judge, with special emphasis on astronomy along the way. It was a dramatic journey that forged an enduring bond between the judge and Wade and became the true genesis for Wade's stellar career.

Now as Director of the Galileo Institute for Advanced Astrophysics, Wade was at the pinnacle of his astronomy career. Returning to Greencastle was a stark reminder of how far he'd come in a short period of time. In many ways his achievements and Clay Arnold's achievements were similarly spectacular, and he looked forward to their meeting.

"I really do think we need to get going," Wade said as they took their final bites of lunch. "They've got me up on the dais with Clay, President Murray, and a couple of the college's trustees. There will be reserved seating up front for you two and Quentin and Luella, plus Clay Arnold's family and friends. Should be a fun group."

With lunch over the three of them climbed into Cassie's car and made the three-minute journey down Franklin and DePauw avenues to the Von Timm Observatory.

When Cassie's car pulled up to the curb by the observatory, Wade got out and murmured to himself, "Hello, old friend." He had returned to a place of very fond memories, and the observatory actually looked even better than he remembered. He was pleased that the college had kept it in good repair.

Immediately President Murray came up to greet Wade and Kayla and made introductions to several college trustees and faculty members. "I just got a call from Clay Arnold," Hannibal Murray said. "They're about five minutes away. Kayla, why don't you and Cassie mingle a bit so Wade and I can go over a couple of things? We'll get started shortly after Clay and his group arrive."

A moment later President Murray felt a sharp tug on his sleeve, and he saw Mortimer Chestnut standing next to him and Wade. "Ahem!" Mortimer made a sound as if to clear his throat and motioned for the president to introduce him to the famous astronomer standing close by.

"Oh, Dr. Henry, I'd like you to meet the chairman of our astronomy department, Dr. Mortimer Chestnut. Mortimer has been looking forward to meeting you."

"It's a pleasure to meet you, Dr. Chestnut," Wade said as he extended his hand. "Your astronomy program has a great history, and my friend, Judge Thaddeus Nathan, would be pleased with the growth of the program."

"Ah, your words honor us all, Dr. Henry," Mortimer replied gushingly. "In fact it is an honor just having you here today for this special occasion."

President Murray was relieved that Dr. Chestnut had not whined about his not being selected to make the presentation to Clay Arnold today. He decided not to risk any potentially awkward conversation with Dr. Chestnut, so he directed Mortimer to go check on the refreshments.

"Refreshments, indeed!" Mortimer muttered bitterly to himself as he walked to the large canopy where the reception would be held. "I'll show that old goat. Push me out of the way, will he?!"

Mortimer decided it was time to send another cryptic e-mail to Clay Arnold to help build the intrigue. He checked his saved files and pressed send: *"Thee or me, Clay Arnold? Which of us will arrive like noble Perseus to save fair Andromeda?"* "Perhaps that message will push Mister Arnold off kilter a bit."

Mortimer was still livid, and he chose to channel his anger and frustration in another direction. He found Wallace Bane and instructed him to go back to his office on campus and pick up his reading glasses.

"But sir, the ceremony will begin momentarily, and I'll miss Dr. Henry's opening remarks if I go now. I've worked so hard to get everything in tip-top shape like you wanted. Can't I please stay, sir? Perhaps Ms. Meemo would be a better person to go since she's familiar with your office."

"You may be right, Mr. Bane, but I want you to do it. Understood?!"

"Yes sir," Wallace replied submissively.

Clarabelle Meemo couldn't help but overhear the exchange between the two men, and she approached Wallace after Dr. Chestnut departed to speak with someone he deemed more important.

"C'mon, Wallace," she said. "I overheard how he treated you, and if we go to the office together, I'm sure we can be back in time."

But being back in time for Wade Henry's opening remarks was not the only thing concerning Wallace the Mole. He knew that his plan to kidnap Maggie Bodine just got much more complicated.

———

Just then our three vehicles pulled up to the curb by the observatory. I exited my Tacoma along with Maggie, Rennie, and Laura. We were followed by Mace, Weed, and Tori exiting Mace's truck. And then right behind them our friend, Assistant Superintendent for the Indiana State Police Trent Reynolds, brought up the rear. His close friend, Abby, was with him. President Murray made a beeline to greet their guest of honor and his friends. Mortimer Chestnut witnessed their arrival from the refreshment area and bristled at all of the attention they were receiving.

"Clay, welcome to Kissinger College!" President Murray said warmly. "We are so pleased to have you with us today. Would you and your guests please come this way? I want you all to meet Wade Henry and his family."

From the refreshment area Dr. Mortimer Chestnut watched as President Murray escorted Clay's entourage towards the dais. He saw three attractive women and noticed that one was blind and that one was a young teenage girl. He intuited that the woman with the auburn hair must be Clay Arnold's lady love, Maggie Bodine.

"Well, well," Mortimer murmured to himself. "Now I need to get her alone somehow and make a clean escape. Then, that Clay Arnold fellow won't feel quite as ebullient on his special day."

He felt for the stun gun hidden in his pocket, and a smirk appeared on his face as his plan began to take shape. "Now, I'll send yet another one of my cryptic e-mails to Mister Arnold just to keep him off balance." And his smirk turned into a sinister leer.

Chapter 17

Ever notice how you meet someone for the first time and you feel an instant positive connection? That's how it was when Wade Henry and I met, and I give President Murray a lot of credit for sensing that this would be the case. My friends and I joined Wade and Kayla Henry in front of the dais, and the Henrys and I made certain that everyone was introduced. If you didn't know better, the scene looked more like a family reunion than an initial meeting.

Both Laura and Rennie were a little shy at first, but that only lasted until Wade made a special point of inviting them to come for a private

behind-the-scenes visit to the Galileo Center for Advanced Astrophysics.

"I know the place where I work has a pretty fancy name," Wade confessed, "but I know where all the fun stuff is, and if you come to see me, I'll make sure you get the really special tour, and we can look through our big telescope as much as you want."

That offer got their attention and immediately made them feel more comfortable. Mace, Weed, and Trent Reynolds were standing on the perimeter listening to the conversations, and I made certain that they didn't feel neglected.

In fact, Wade was delighted when I told him that Weed had attended MIT for his undergraduate education, and that led them to discover that they had alumni and faculty friends in common from their college days. Kayla, Maggie, and Tori hit it off from the start, and they looked forward to talking more after the award ceremony.

From his perch by the refreshment area, Mortimer Chestnut eyed the cozy spectacle unfolding in front of him, and he slipped his hand inside his pocket to touch his stun gun in an effort to calm himself. He kept his eyes glued on Maggie Bodine as he muttered to himself, "Soon enough. Just be smart about this, Mortie, my boy."

Just then Wallace "the Mole" Bane and Clarabelle Meemo came rushing up to him. Wallace had a pained expression on his face as he told his boss that he couldn't find his reading glasses in his office.

"We looked everywhere," Wallace cried. "Ms. Meemo came with me, but neither of us was able to find your glasses, sir."

"Not to worry, Mr. Bane, I discovered that I had them in my jacket all along. Silly me."

Clarabelle shot her boss a look that could melt steel, and she lightly patted Wallace on his shoulder to offer some consolation.

"Well, I have some last minute details that I must attend to," Wallace said, and he immediately withdrew to hide his embarrassment and frustration.

"Why did you do that?" Ms. Meemo said with undisguised vitriol in her voice. "That man works his heart out for you and the college, and you treat him like a slave."

Mortimer was taken aback by her directness. "Now, now, Ms. Meemo, it was a simple mistake, and besides, what's he going to do about it?" he snidely replied.

Wallace went downstairs to his office beneath the observatory and sat at his desk as he tried to regain his composure. He felt hurt and humiliated. His only consolation was that Clarabelle had been a friend to him when he needed one. Regardless, he felt compelled to try and pull off kidnapping Maggie Bodine during the interlude between the ceremony and the reception. He still felt stung by Clay Arnold being named Astrophotographer of the Year and receiving an honorary doctorate from his college. No, this was something he needed to do to protect the waning vestiges of his own self worth.

"There you are," Wallace said as he reached inside his desk and pulled out a plastic baggie containing a cloth saturated in the ether he had gotten from the chemistry department. He placed the baggie in his jacket pocket and looked heavenward. He got up from his desk and glanced toward the hidden storeroom. This was the moment he had been waiting for. Wallace closed his office door, took a deep breath, and returned to watch the events upstairs and await his opportunity.

President Murray stood proudly at the podium and asked everyone in attendance to please take their seats. It was a glorious fall afternoon, and the sun was already beginning to dip a bit in the western sky. Hannibal Murray watched patiently as folks took their seats, and he thought about a time in the not-too-distant future when he would no longer preside over such special events as the college president. Retirement was on the horizon.

"It gives me enormous pleasure to welcome you here today for two very special reasons. First, because this event recognizes a true master of his art, Clay Arnold, and it also gives Kissinger College an opportunity to welcome home a very special native son, Wade Henry." A robust round of applause ensued, and Clay and Wade looked over at each other and nodded approvingly.

"Now before I introduce Wade Henry who will present the honorary doctorate to Clay Arnold, there are a few people who I would also like to recognize."

President Murray introduced three of the college's trustees who were in attendance, and he then asked all of Clay and Wade's family members and friends to stand and be recognized. More applause. Rennie and Laura couldn't help but giggle a little at the attention, and Maggie knew from their reaction that bringing Laura to Greencastle and Indy was a perfect thing to do.

Mortimer Chestnut had moved away from his perch at the refreshment area and had sidled over closer to where Maggie Bodine was seated. His eyes were so glued on her that he almost wet his pants when President Murray said, "I also wish to thank Dr. Mortimer Chestnut, chairman of the department of astrophysics for the fine efforts that he and his staff have made to help bring this ceremony to fruition."

Mortimer beamed awkwardly like a cheshire cat who had nearly been caught with his paws in the goldfish bowl. Clarabelle and Wallace looked at each other knowing that they were the ones who really deserved the credit.

"It's okay, Wallace," Clarabelle said. "President Murray knows who really did the work." Wallace looked at her quizzically. "He does?"

"And so, ladies and gentlemen," President Murray continued, "it gives me profound pleasure to introduce a true star in the field of astrophysics; a man whose parents were devoted to the best ideals of Kissinger College; a man whose vision has allowed countless others to see and witness the grandeur of the universe . . . please welcome the Director of the Galileo Institute for Advanced Astrophysics, Dr. Wade Henry."

Kayla Henry looked over at her mother-in-law, Cassie, and saw tears of joy at her son's recognition. "His father would've been so proud of Wade," Cassie said to Kayla. "Judge Nathan, too. Thaddeus was Wade's true north star when his father was murdered, and he needed adult male guidance and friendship."

Wade approached the podium, and he and President Murray posed for a couple of photos amid the amplitude of approving applause.

Wade looked out over the collection of faces in the audience and began speaking. "Thank you President Murray for your kind words and your very warm welcome to Kissinger College. It's great to be back home, and to reconnect with friends and this great observatory again. I know that my wife, Kayla, and my mother, Cassie, join me in expressing our sincere appreciation for being asked to participate today, especially in presenting Clay Arnold with the recognition he so richly deserves."

Wade paused briefly to collect his thoughts. He glanced at his prepared notes and decided instead to slip them in his jacket pocket. He began again.

"A lot of years have passed since I stood on this very ground with Judge Thaddeus Nathan. To return today after my teenage years is very emotional for me. Back then I never dreamed of having a career in astronomy. It's funny how things work out."

Wade looked over at Kayla and his mother in the front row. The audience was respectfully quiet. "After my dad was murdered, I felt like I had lost my way. I believe the judge felt the same way with his Ellie's death. On more than one occasion he advised me to look to the stars for comfort. He also encouraged me to be 'renaissance-like' when considering the universe, and by that he meant to embrace both the artistic and the scientific aspects of the cosmos.

"Upon his death, when he endowed the astronomy program here at Kissinger College, it was a clarion call for me to remember his advice and to build a career around the stars." Wade took a pregnant pause and began again.

"Like many of you, I have been familiar with Clay Arnold's photography for a number of years. Often Kayla and I have sat together and looked at books of images that Clay shot . . . some were poignant street scenes, others were great nature shots from across the globe . . . fashion and design and portrait work . . . many were so artfully composed as to appear magical. And then, he discovered the night sky which gave him a brave new world to explore. And so we are gathered here today to pay tribute to Clay Arnold's magnificent career, his stunning astral images, and to recall Judge Thaddeus Nathan's advice to embrace the artistic as well as the scientific."

The audience applauded Wade's heartfelt sentiments. From their perches at the rear of the seating area, both Mortimer Chestnut and Wallace Bane were like birds of prey watching Maggie Bodine, waiting for their chance to fly into action. Unwitting competitors for the same prize. Mortimer edged even closer to the front row and cast a glance over to the panel van that he had parked a few feet from the rear of the observatory. Wallace also moved closer to where Maggie was seated but on the opposite side of the seating area from Mortimer's location. Both men felt inside their pockets for the devices they would use to subdue Maggie. Timing and a little luck were critical for each.

Wade Henry asked me to join him at the dais, and he placed the Thaddeus Nathan Medallion around my neck while President Murray read the proclamation awarding me with an Honorary Doctorate of Humanities. It was a very humbling experience, and I smiled proudly at Maggie and Laura and my family of friends. And now it was my turn to speak.

"First, I wish to thank President Murray and everyone associated with Kissinger College for this wonderful recognition. While I never had an opportunity to know Judge Thaddeus Nathan, I feel that I have had a glimpse into his legendary character thanks to Wade Henry's words. It is indeed an honor to receive the Nathan Medallion and the Honorary Doctorate of Humanities. I also want to thank Wade for being here today. His presence adds even greater significance to this special occasion, and I am grateful beyond words."

I paused for a few moments to collect my next thoughts and then spoke, "I'm not an astrophysicist. I'm not a scientist. I daresay that the faculty and staff in the college's astronomy program have probably forgotten more about the cosmos than I've ever known. I'm a photographer, and someone who only relatively recently gazed upon the night sky with artistic interest."

These honest words caught Wallace by surprise, and he appreciated Clay's frankness. Regardless, he remained poised to take action. Mortimer Chestnut, on the other hand, could've cared less about honesty and frankness. All he wanted to do was stun and kidnap Maggie Bodine so he could later position himself as a Perseus-like hero to set her free. If he could accomplish that, then he thought that Kissinger's board of trustees would see him as a capable leader for the school. It was a simple plan, and he awaited his chance to act.

I continued. "I am not a man of God. I mean no disrespect in saying that. It's just how I am, but when I look up into the night sky, it is so vast and wondrous that it does indeed border on the theological for me. Like many of you, and Wade Henry as well, I have suffered great personal loss. Somehow trying to capture the grandeur of the heavens with photographs helps bring me an odd sense of reassurance . . . that we are all part of something truly magnificent if we only avail ourselves to it in our own way."

I paused briefly and began again. "I can't adeqautely tell you how special this is for me to receive an honorary doctorate from Kissinger College, and also receiving my recent recognition as Astrophotographer of the Year from *Space and Beyond* magazine. Either of those would be a capstone in a person's career, and so I feel doubly blessed. In the days leading up to being here, I tried to come up with remarks that would be poignant and worthy of someone receiving an honorary doctorate. I've frankly been a little nervous because I couldn't find the right words, that is until I heard Wade relate Judge Nathan's sage advice . . . to embrace both the scientific and the artistic aspects of the cosmos. I guess I would go a step closer than the cosmos and encourage each of us to embrace the scientific and the artistic in our daily lives. It's what I try to achieve in my photography, and I am delighted and humbled by your thoughtful recognition of my efforts."

I wrapped up my comments by thanking President Murray and Kissinger College again and recognizing Wade Henry for his great participation. I looked at the front row and saw Maggie and Laura and my family of friends smiling at me. I felt that this honorary degree meant as much to each of them as it did to me. I ended by saying that I looked forward to visiting with folks during the reception.

At that, Dr. Mortimer Chestnut sidled even closer to where Maggie Bodine was standing. Still wearing the medallion, I made a beeline to Maggie and was greeted by a hug and kiss that I have come to know and love. Mortimer slinked a few feet away but remained cautiously alert. His panel van was parked behind the refreshment area. Laura and Rennie made a dash for cake and lemonade, and Weed, Tori, and Mace went to chat more with Wade Henry and Kayla and Cassie. And Wallace Bane watched and waited for Clay and Maggie to separate long enough for him to lead her away and use the ether.

But Clay and Maggie did not separate. They were arm in arm the whole time. "So, how'd I do?" I asked Maggie unabashedly looking for even more adoring adulation.

"You were great, Doctor Arnold. Handsome, erudite, sincere, and, of course, brilliant!"

"Thanks, Maggie. I'm so glad you're here. It really wouldn't have been the same for me if you hadn't been."

Then I added a little levity. "Getting all of that praise has worked up an appetite for me. Do you want to get some refreshments?"

"Sure," she said, "but let's leave room for a 'snack' later on, too!" I caught her drift. We walked arm-in-arm toward the refreshments and a small throng of people who were waiting to talk with us.

Mortimer stalked them like a hungry beast, and Wallace followed at a safe distance from the other direction. They were so intent on their prey that neither was aware of the other's presence.

Rennie and Laura had both gotten a piece of cake and went to sit under a shady tree. "Hey,

Laura," Rennie said. "Do you want some lemonade? I'll go and get it for us if you want. I'll be back in a flash."

Independently, Mortimer and Wallace saw that getting Maggie Bodine alone was going to be nearly impossible. Wallace moaned to himself when he realized that there was a very good chance that he wouldn't be able to pull off his kidnapping. Regardless, he pulled the baggie containing the ether and held it in his hand hidden beneath a paper plate. Wallace moved to within ten feet of Maggie and Clay. He knew he had to get her alone somehow.

Mortimer was now within a few feet of the couple also, and he had his stun gun at the ready. Just then President Murray joined Maggie and Clay and asked if he could prevail upon them to be photographed with some of the college's dignitaries and guests. They walked back toward the dais, and both Wallace and Mortimer slumped as they saw their last chance to grab Maggie vanish before their eyes. Wallace slipped the ether back into his pocket and withdrew into the background to lick his wounds and think about what might have been.

"Aaarrraaggghhh!" Mortimer growled through clenched teeth. "I haven't done all of this planning for nothing," he muttered to himself. He noticed the crowd in the refreshment area begin to thin out as guests wandered over to where the photos were being taken.

And then, Mortimer noticed that the teenage girl, Laura, was seated under a tree by herself. A thought flashed in his mind, and he quickly surveyed the area to see if anyone was close by. He walked up to Laura, and with his frosty smile said, "Oh miss, your Aunt Maggie has asked me to see if you would be willing to help bring a little surprise over to Clay."

"Surprise?!" Laura said quizzically. "Aunt Maggie didn't mention a surprise to me."

"I understand, dear," Mortimer said. "It was a last minute thing, and it'll only take a sec. Would you please come with me behind the refreshment area?"

Laura looked to see where Rennie was and noticed he was still in line for their lemonade. "Okay, sure," she said, and she got up and followed Dr. Chestnut in the direction he was leading. Mortimer quickly gave the area a visual scan and saw that everyone was moving toward the dais again. When they were finally out of view, Mortimer said, "Oh gee, look there's your aunt now." Laura instinctively turned to look and Mortimer discharged his stun gun into her side and caught her limp but twitching body as she slumped into his arms.

In a flash, Mortimer looked around and saw that no one had noticed. He then scooped her up, awkwardly waddled the ten feet to his waiting panel van, slid the side door open, and tossed her inside. Ten seconds later he was behind the wheel and slowly driving along DePauw Avenue away from the festivities at the Von Timm Observatory.

A few moments after that Rennie returned to the tree where he had left Laura and wondered where she went.

Chapter 18

Mortimer Chestnut whistled a nonsensical tune as he drove through Greencastle's courthouse square and turned north on State Route 231. He pulled into a vacant parking lot near the Putnam County Museum and went to the rear of the van to check on his unconscious passenger. Just in case she regained lucidity, he climbed into the rear of the vehicle and gagged and securely tied her up with duct tape.

"Now just a little bit further, my dear, and we'll have you to your new home," he said out loud to the unresponsive girl. "If I couldn't snatch Maggie

Bodine away from Clay Arnold, I think you'll do just as nicely, maybe even better."

Mortimer continued to drive up Waterworks Hill and turned left onto County Road 100. He was now entering the fringe of the Putnam County countryside and breathed a sigh of relief that he had made it out of town unnoticed.

"Hmmm, I wonder how long it'll take for Clay Arnold and his friends to notice that the girl is missing," he mused to himself. "Oh, I'd love to be a fly on the wall for that startling revelation!"

Mortimer drove three miles along curvy country roads, periodically checking his rearview mirror to see if he had anyone following. Aside from a couple of grain trucks being filled with corn, the landscape was quiet. A few minutes later Mortimer turned west on County Road 250 and came to a stop at the bush-shrouded entrance to his hideaway. He got out, unlocked the metal gate, and pulled the panel van inside. He got out again, relocked the gate, and drove the final hundred yards to his secluded cabin. His passenger was still unconscious.

"I did it!" he exclaimed with unbridled glee. "I actually pulled it off, and nobody is the wiser. Take that, President Hannibal Murray! And you too, Clay Arnold! Good ol' Mortie boy just got the better of you smart-ass celebrities."

Mortimer opened his cabin door and with great effort managed to get Laura into the basement room that he had prepared. "Ah, home sweet home," Mortimer laughed as he deposited Laura's limp form on to the cot inside. He nudged her leg with the tip of his shoe and saw that she was beginning to re-gain consciousness. He exited the room and locked the door behind himself and went back upstairs to turn on the cabin's surveillance system. "Tip-top!" he proudly said to himself. I think I'll make a tip-top college president, indeed!"

Rennie looked for Laura around the refreshment area and the grounds of the Von Timm Observatory. She was nowhere to be found.

"Dang girl, where'd you go?" a bewildered Rennie said out loud. He went inside the observatory to look there but no luck. He came outside and saw Mace, Weed, and Tori watching Clay interact with his admirers. Maggie was with him.

"I can't find Laura. Have you seen her?!" Rennie asked his friends breathlessly. "I looked all around here and inside the observatory. I even waited by the ladies room. I mean, I can't find her anywhere!"

"Easy lad," Mace said. "I'm sure she'll turn up." Then Mace leaned over to Weed and said, "Maybe we should go find Trent Reynolds and see if he can light a fire under the college's security detail."

"Good idea," Weed said. "He's over there by his car with Abby. Let's go."

"Rennie, why don't you hang with Tori for a few minutes. We'll be right back."

Trent Reynolds took his work very seriously, and when Weed and Mace expressed their concerns about Laura's absence, Trent immediately radioed his dispatcher to contact campus security for additional help. He also contacted Sheriff Hatfield in the Putnam County Sheriff's office who said he was on his way.

"I know she's only been gone a few minutes, but if you guys think this is serious, then I do, too."

"Thanks, Trent," Weed said. "Our instincts tell us something's wrong, though, right Mace?"

Mace nodded his agreement. Just then another campus security car pulled up to the curb and three officers got out and came up to Trent. They got a description of Laura and what she was wearing. At Trent's suggestion, the officers set up a security perimeter and began searching the residential yards around the observatory.

Clay's throng of admirers were beginning to thin out, and he and Maggie spent a few more minutes talking with Wade and Kayla Henry. Wade suggested that there could be some fascinating astrophotography work that Clay might want to fit into his schedule at the Galileo Institute. Wade's team had just unveiled their latest major telescope, and he wanted an artist's eye to help capture some new worlds. They agreed to keep in touch.

After the Henrys left, Clay noticed Weed motioning for him to come over.

"I think something may be amiss," Clay whispered to Maggie as he pointed in Weed and Mace's direction. They walked across the yard to join them.

"What's up?!" Clay asked when he got there.

"We can't find Laura," Weed said to Clay and Maggie.

"What do you mean you can't find Laura?!" Maggie asked with genuine concern. "She was with Rennie just a couple of minutes ago."

Rennie heard her and said, "She was, Maggie. I left her by that tree and went to get lemonade for us, but when I got back, she was gone."

"Laura! Laura!" Maggie called out, but there was no reply. "Oh no, this can't be happening! Laura! Laura!" She looked at Clay with fear in her eyes.

"We'll find her, Maggie. I promise," Clay said.

Over the next few minutes Clay and his friends went off in different directions looking for the missing girl. Weed and Mace went inside the observatory and took the stairs down toward Wallace Bane's office.

"We're looking for a teenage girl named Laura." They saw Wallace's name badge and asked him if he'd seen her.

"I'm sorry, gentlemen, but I've been down here for a while, and no one has ventured down here."

"Would you please help us search the area? Campus security is here, but you undoubtedly know the immediate area better than most."

Wallace felt complimented by Mace's remark and said, "Of course, I'll come right away."

At this point Maggie was growing frantic about her missing niece. "My god, what will I say to my sister?" she asked Clay.

Just then Trent Reynolds and Lucas Benedix, the director of Kissinger College's security department, came up to report.

Mr. Benedix said, "Nothing solid to report yet. I've got my officers searching the area, and I contacted the Greencastle Police Department and Mike Hatfield at the Putnam County Sheriff's office. We went ahead and issued a county-wide BOLO. Frankly, with Trent here from the state police, everyone is leaping into action." Mr. Benedix turned to Maggie and said, "We'll do everything we can, ma'am, to get Laura back. Hopefully it's just a prank or something, but I assure you we're all taking it very seriously."

Clay felt his mobile phone vibrate in his pocket and looked at the e-mail message that appeared.

"Uh guys," Clay said somberly. "You might want to take a look at this."

"I have your sweet Andromeda, Dr. Arnold," the message read. *"Let's see who the true hero is . . . thee or me . . ."*

Chapter 19

Trent Reynolds reached for Clay's cell phone, and he and Sheriff Hatfield looked at the message.

"Well, I guess we just answered the question about Laura's disappearance," Trent said. "It would appear that Laura's been kidnapped."

"That might explain some of the other e-mails I recently received, too," Clay submitted. "I didn't take the others seriously since I get a lot of spam, but now I think they're all related."

The two officers scanned through Clay's inbox and saw the other e-mails he referenced. Trent immediately called Rebecca Willett, his associate at the Indiana State Police.

"Rebecca, we've got a probable kidnapping in progress here in Greencastle. I want to forward some messages that Clay Arnold received on his cell phone. I'd like you to see what, if anything, you can glean from them, and I think it would be a good idea for you to hightail it down here and work closely with the local authorities. We don't have a lot to go on yet, and I'm hopeful that your computer savvy will help shed some light on this. Time's important."

"On my way, Trent," Rebecca said. "When I get the e-mails, I'll have our cyber security folks see if they can come up with the identity of the sender."

Maggie was stunned that Laura could be snatched right from under their noses. "Clay, I've got to call my sister, but I swear I don't know what to tell her. Laura is their only child, and my sister and her husband think that the sun rises and sets on her."

"We'll get her back, Maggie, I promise you. Trent and his staff are as good as they come." But, I hadn't really convinced myself of that yet. I know how evil some folks are. That's why I became an avenging vigilante in the first place. Trent and I made eye contact, and we knew we had a very dangerous situation with no clear positive end in sight. Now the true detective work would begin.

Laura finally regained full use of her body and faculties but was in a state of shock and had trouble comprehending where she was and why she was locked up. Within the dankness of her crude room, she screamed for help at the top of her lungs.

A few minutes later a vaguely familiar voice came from the other side of the strong wooden door. "Now, now, Miss Andromeda, no one will hear you screaming so you might as well get used to that!"

"My name is not Andromeda. Why are you doing this to me?" Laura cried. "I want to go home. Why won't you let me go?"

"Soon enough, my little Andromeda, soon enough, but for now you need to behave. There is water in the sink, and a toilet if you need to go potty. I will bring you something to eat in a little while if you calm down."

Laura heard her captor's muffled footsteps as he walked away from her door. Her eyes were beginning to adjust to the bare lightbulb, and she shuffled over to the sink for a drink of water. It had an eggy sulfur taste to it, but was soothing on her parched throat from screaming.

Mortimer Chestnut returned upstairs to the comfort of his living quarters. He double-checked his perimeter security system and sat down at his computer to contemplate his next steps.

"Well, Mortie my boy," he said to himself. "You certainly made the best of a disappointing situation at the observatory, and now you have to decide on the best way to return this darn kid and look like a hero."

Mortimer spent several minutes looking at his computer confirming that he had structured the source of his e-mails in such a way as to implicate Wallace "the Mole" Bane as the girl's abductor. He also wanted to continue to annoy Clay Arnold with his antagonistic messages.

"So, Doctor Clay Arnold, it would seem that Kissinger College will give an honorary doctorate to just about anyone, eh?! Your sweet Andromeda has been screaming and carrying on something awful since I snatched her away from you and Ms. Bodine. So sad to hear someone so young and pretty crying and begging. Do you really think you can save her?" Mortimer Chestnut reviewed his message and pressed the send button. "That should push Dr. Arnold over the edge!"

With the festivities over at the Von Timm Observatory, Clay suggested to Weed and Mace that they take Tori and Rennie and return home to the brewery complex. They reluctantly agreed. "We're just a phone call away," Mace consoled. "Let us know if there's anything we can do to help."

"Thanks, Mace." Clay replied. "Obviously Maggie and I will stay here in Greencastle to work with Trent and the local authorities. I'm not sure when we'll get back home."

A few moments later, Clay saw that he had another message from their cocky adversary. He shared it with Trent Reynolds and Sheriff Hatfield and tried to hide it from Maggie, but she insisted on seeing it. Her knees buckled when she read the part about Laura screaming and crying and begging.

"This guy sure likes to taunt us," Trent said. "And, what's all of this stuff about referring to Laura as Andromeda?"

"I'm not an expert of classical mythology," Clay admitted. "If my memory serves me correctly, though, Andromeda was the daughter of King Cepheus and Queen Cassiopeia. The Queen had boasted that she was more beautiful than even the Nereids who were vain sea nymphs. As the story goes, the Nereids were upset by Cassiopeia's insult, and they implored Neptune, god of the seas, to teach her a lesson. Neptune had their daughter, Andromeda, chained to a rock so that the sea monster, Cetus, could devour her. But Perseus, fresh from slaying the gorgon, Medusa, arrived on his winged horse, Pegasus, and saved Andromeda from certain death. At least, that's how the myth goes," Clay concluded.

"So, it would appear," Trent said, "that our kidnapper is well-versed in both astronomy and mythology. Now we just need to figure out who's angry enough to commit a capital crime."

From a safe distance, Wallace Bane couldn't help but overhear their conversation. Given the number of police officers scouring the neighborhood, he actually felt relieved that he hadn't been able to snatch Maggie Bodine like he'd intended. He was also very relieved that his boss, Dr. Chestnut, had left on vacation as soon as Clay received his doctorate. "Thank goodness Dr. Chestnut isn't here to make my life even more miserable," Wallace said to himself.

Several minutes later a car with state license plates pulled up to the observatory, and Trent's assistant, Rebecca Willett, emerged and walked over to him and Clay and Maggie.

"Rebecca, it's good to see you again," Clay said. "I want you to meet Maggie Bodine."

"Good to see you, too, Clay, and to meet you, Ms. Bodine. I sure wish it were under more pleasant circumstances."

Trent asked Rebecca, "Have you and the cyber team had a chance to get any leads on the kidnapper yet? We just got another quirky message from someone we believe is the kidnapper, and I just forwarded it on to you as you were pulling up. It should be in your inbox now. President Murray has also offered the college's information technology staff and Dr. Chestnut's assistant, Clarabelle Meemo, to help work with our people.

"Have we received a ransom note yet?" Rebecca asked.

"No ransom note. Just these unusual e-mails about mythological people."

"I'll go see what I can find out from the college's IT staff," Rebecca said and she hurried off to connect with them.

At this point Maggie was feeling overwhelmed with anxiety, and she leaned heavily into Clay for support. "Will you please stay with me while I call my sister?" she asked Clay. "I usually feel that I can handle most things, but I've never been so scared in my life."

"C'mon," Clay said. "Let's go inside the observatory so you can have some privacy." On the way in they saw an unusual looking fellow whose name badge read *Wallace Bane*. Mr. Bane opened the door for them and bowed submissively as they walked by him.

"Please feel free to use my office downstairs if you need to," Mr. Bane offered.

Maggie's sister nearly had a stroke when Maggie told her about Laura's abduction. She said that she and Laura's father would immediately try to charter a direct flight to Greencastle's tiny airport. It would be a few hours before they could arrive, though.

Maggie assured her sister that the authorities were doing everything humanly possible to get Laura back safely. Maggie promised to keep her apprised of any new information as it became available.

Once outside the Von Timm Observatory again, Trent approached Clay and Maggie. "President Murray has secured a room for you two at the Walden Inn. It doesn't seem that there's much you can do here right now. Why don't you go and get some rest? You're going to need to stay in good shape for this ordeal, and I promise to let you know the minute we learn anything, okay? I need to get back to Indianapolis right now, but Rebecca is fully capable of handling things for us here."

Maggie reluctantly agreed, and a campus security officer drove them the few blocks to the Walden Inn and helped get them checked in.

When they finally arrived inside their room, Maggie finally fell into Clay's arms and broke down into tears. "Never in a million years could I have guessed that something like this could happen," Maggie sobbed. "Laura is so special, and the thought of her being scared and in danger is heartbreaking to me. What are we going to do, Clay?"

I held her for the longest time and tried to be as consoling as possible, but I knew we had a very frightening situation. "There's not much else we can do right now. Trent's officers and the local police departments are working hard. As long as this guy keeps communicating with us, we have a shot at getting to him and getting Laura back safely."

"Oh Clay, I would do anything right now to have Laura back. I feel so guilty for putting her in harm's way."

"Maggie, you didn't put her in harm's way. If anyone did, it was me. Apparently, the abductor has some issue with me and my receiving the honorary doctorate. But even still, neither of us is responsible for this guy kidnapping Laura. Sometimes bad stuff happens, and it's not going to do either of us, or Laura, any good with the self-recriminations."

"Believe me, Maggie," I said gravely, "I am very capable of taking matters into my own hands, but right now we need to stay focused and let the authorities do their work."

Maggie looked me directly in the eye and said, "Right now, Clay, if the authorities can't get Laura back soon, I think I would be very comfortable with you taking matters into your own hands, and I don't even know what that means exactly."

"I understand," Maggie. "I'm not sure I want you to know what it means exactly because I don't want to frighten you. It's something I've wanted to discuss with you for a very long time, and I've frankly been too nervous about how you'd react."

Maggie looked at me, not so much with concern, but more with a detached curiosity. "Have you done things worse than what you did to that guy's motorcycle in Moab?"

"Yes," I said evenly. And then I said, "Much worse and more than once."

"Well, this certainly has been a day full of surprises," she said. "All we need now is for a meteor to hit the planet, and the day will be complete!" And then she did a surprising thing. She softened, just a little.

"I don't want to know details, Clay. I know you well enough to know that you must've had your reasons, and all I want is to get Laura back any way we can."

"Thank you, Maggie, I can't tell you how much of a relief this is to me, but I want you to understand why I've done some of the things I've done, and where I am now."

The lights in the room were off and the late afternoon sun cast soothing shadows across the bed where we now lay. I stared at the ceiling and began, "When Jennifer was murdered in the Planned Parenthood bombing in Broadripple, I was totally consumed by rage and grief. If it hadn't been for Weed, Tori, Mace, and Rennie, I don't know what might've become of me. I didn't particularly seek out people I wanted gone, but I had no moral qualms about eliminating right-wing nut cases and nasty criminals, either. I felt like I was an avenging vigilante, and I wanted to even the score for people who couldn't defend themselves."

In the dimming light I felt Maggie's eyes looking at me, and I turned to face her. A flash of waning sunlight caught her auburn hair and highlighted the emerald green cast of her eyes.

I continued, "There's something else you need to know. Aside from the biker in Moab, I haven't done anything violent since we had the incidents with the Hacker men a year ago. And trust me, there are still times when I feel my blood boil, and I want to nail someone who truly deserves it, like this jerk who grabbed Laura."

"Honestly, though," I continued, "being with you, Maggie, has helped calm the savage beast inside me, as cliche as that sounds. I don't feel the rage quite the same way I used to. Now, I just want to be a great partner to you. I want to be a loving member of my small family of friends. I still want to be a great photographer, and I want to be a positive force for good in the world around me. And right now, what I want more than anything is for us to get Laura back safely."

Maggie moved even closer to me and held me tightly. "Oh Clay," she sighed, "I just want everything to be okay. I'm scared, and I'm tired, but I also know how much I trust you. Can we please just hold each other for a while?"

And that's what we did.

Chapter 20

"I THINK WE HAVE something," Rebecca Willett told Trent over the phone. "I've been working closely with our ISP tech guys and the IT folks at Kissinger College, and I think we've discovered a backdoor into the college's e-mail system."

"Excellent news!" Trent said. "Is it pointing to anyone in particular?"

"Yeah, it sure seems to," Rebecca said. "It appears that a series of e-mails were scheduled to drop on command from a computer belonging to an employee in the astronomy department. A guy named Wallace Bane. We've been in touch with President Murray's office. He's heading back to the

Von Timm Observatory now. Apparently that's where Mr. Bane's office is located. Unfortunately, we have not been able to locate Mr. Bane's immediate supervisor, Dr. Mortimer Chestnut. Dr. Chestnut's assistant, Clarabelle Meemo, said that he went on vacation at the conclusion of today's ceremony and reception."

Trent was about to tell Rebecca to bring Mr. Bane in, but she anticipated his directive. "We're already on it, boss. We have campus security personnel and two Putnam County officers going to pay Mr. Bane a visit."

"Good work, Rebecca. Let me know how it goes with Bane. I'll call Clay and Maggie and let them know we're making some progress."

Wallace Bane puttered around his office not really doing much of anything. He was lost in thought about the events of the day and his failure to kidnap Maggie Bodine. He had so wanted to teach that astro-wannabe, Clay Arnold, a lesson.

"It's the story of my life. One more bite out of the pie of mediocrity. I suppose it's better this way. I certainly never wanted to hurt her . . . just, just get a little attention and prove that I, Wallace-the-Mole-Bane, could pull something like that off."

"Oh well," Wallace mused, "At least my pesky boss, Mortimer, is gone for a while. Surely, he can't humiliate me while he's on vacation. I might as well accept the reality that I will live out my days here at Kissinger College in total anonymity."

There was no advance warning. No phone call. No text message. No polite knock on the door. There came a splintering crash against Wallace's office door, and four officers surrounded him as he sat at his desk.

"Where is she, Mr. Bane?" Sheriff Mike Hatfield demanded. "Where's the girl?"

"What, what!" Wallace stammered. "What girl? There's some mistake, Sheriff."

The officers unhooked Wallace's computer and carried it out the door, while the others rifled through his desk to look for incriminating evidence.

"It'll go a lot easier on you, Mr. Bane, if you cooperate," Sheriff Hatfield said.

"But I am cooperating, sir . . ." Wallace managed to say.

"Sheriff, you might want to take a look at this," one of the officers said.

They slid the bookcase away from the wall revealing the door to the hidden storeroom where Wallace had intended hold Maggie. Sheriff Hatfield went inside the dim space and saw the chains that were attached to the wall. Wallace's heart sank when the sheriff emerged from the room and Wallace saw the look in his eye.

"Where's the girl, Mr. Bane?" he asked again. We know you sent several e-mails to Clay Arnold taunting him. We know you had opportunity since you work here. As for motive, I don't think we should have too much trouble figuring that out. It doesn't appear that you have that many positive character witnesses."

"But, I can explain," Wallace pleaded, but he knew that the evidence didn't look promising to his case. "And what e-mails? I don't know anything about sending e-mails to Clay Arnold. There must be some mistake!"

At that, the security personnel lifted Mr. Bane from his chair and handcuffed him. They led him upstairs to the main level of the observatory and then outdoors. As Wallace was dragged along to a waiting squad car, his eyes briefly met Clarabelle's, and he averted his gaze in shame and embarrassment. She was standing next to her uncle, President Murray, and clung to his arm as she saw her friend being hauled off to jail.

Clay and Maggie arrived on the scene just as an officer was lowering Wallace's head beneath a squad car's door frame. He sat alone in the back seat staring straight ahead. Maggie went up to look at him through the glass and tears rolled down her cheeks. "Please!" she called out to Wallace. "Where is she? Please!" Wallace just stared straight ahead, and a tear rolled down his cheek as well.

Clay gently guided Maggie away from the car, and they walked toward Rebecca who was standing near the entrance to the observatory. She was on the phone with Trent.

"Yeah, we just apprehended Mr. Bane, and he's being transported to the county jail for questioning. He hasn't been charged with anything yet, but from the evidence we've seen so far, it looks pretty incriminating. I've got Clay and Maggie walking up to me right now, so unless you want to talk with them, I should probably hang up."

"Okay, you're good to go. I've got more than I can handle right now in Indy, but I appreciate your keeping me informed. Keep the pressure on Mr. Bane. We've got to get Maggie's niece back quickly. My experience is that the longer things drag on in a kidnapping case, the outcome rarely improves. Please tell Clay and Maggie I'll be in touch soon." They finished their call.

Clay asked Rebecca about the suspect they had in custody. "So, who's that in the squad car? I remember seeing him earlier in the day." Sheriff Hatfield joined Rebecca and said, "His name is Wallace Bane. He has worked in the astronomy department for many years according to the information we just got from Human Resources. The strange thing is that very few people on faculty knew him because his office is at the Von Timm Observatory rather than being on the main campus. Apparently, he's called the Mole because he rarely surfaces from his office below ground level."

"Sounds like a bleak existence," Rebecca commented. "Not surprising that a loner like him might feel isolated and frustrated. But I don't want to get ahead of ourselves yet on this investigation. We can't just assume that he's our abductor. We need to question him thoroughly and follow the evidence."

Just then Hannibal Murray and Clarabelle Meemo came up to them and asked about Mr. Bane's apprehension. Sheriff Hatfield repeated what he had just said to Clay and Maggie, but Clarabelle was skeptical.

"This just doesn't seem right to me," Clarabelle said. "I know that Wallace is an unusual fellow, but I've gotten to know him while we were preparing for today's ceremony, and I just don't see him as the sort of man who would do something like this."

"I appreciate your comments," Rebecca said, "but between the incriminating e-mails that were sent to Clay from his computer and that makeshift dungeon he had hidden behind his office, he has a lot of explaining to do. Why don't you come with us to the county lockup and see if you can get him to tell us what he knows about Laura?"

"I can do that," Clarabelle said. She looked over at President Murray who motioned for her to go with the officers. "Oh, and by the way," President Murray said, "where is Dr. Chestnut? He should be here."

"I thought he told you he was going on vacation," Clarabelle said.

"Vacation?!" her uncle the president blurted. "The academic year just started, and he's going on vacation. See if you can get him back here pronto!"

"I tried to reach him again a few minutes ago, sir, but he's not answering his phone, and he didn't say where he was going."

President Murray's face began to turn red with irritation, and he directed his niece to keep trying to reach him. Clarabelle left with Rebecca and Sheriff Hatfield, and President Murray turned to Clay and Maggie. "I am so sorry that this has happened, Maggie. I hope you know we're doing everything humanly possible to get Laura back, and Clay, I'm so sorry that this has dampened what was supposed to be a very special day for you here."

"Thank you," Maggie said. "Clay and I know everyone's concerned. It's just so frightening. I can't imagine what that poor child is going through." She shuddered at the thought.

Just then Clay's cell phone vibrated again, and he saw that he had another message. It was similar to the previous taunts he'd received. *"Oh Doctor Arnold, Princess Andromeda is weeping. She's so scared and alone. Is there anyone who could possibly save her?"*

Maggie's knees buckled when she read the message over Clay's shoulder. He caught her and seated her on a nearby chair. Clay immediately forwarded the new message to Trent, Rebecca, and Sheriff Hatfield.

Maggie spoke up, "But if that message came from the kidnapper, and they have Wallace in custody, who sent that message?"

"Good question," Clay said. "But we have to remember that the previous messages appeared to have been timed for impact. This could be just another scheduled message that didn't require Bane to actually click "Send". On the other hand, Maggie may be correct. Wallace Bane may have just been a ruse, and the real abductor is still out there. And, if that's the case, where do we go from here?"

Chapter 21

WALLACE BANE SAT ALONE in a holding cell at the Putnam County jail. He was bewildered by the recent turn of events in his life. First, he planned for weeks to wreak his sense of justice on that upstart astrophotographer, Clay Arnold, by snatching his girlfriend. Then, that plan failed out of pure happenstance. That was followed by his being apprehended for a crime he didn't commit. And to top it off, the police found his hidden storeroom cell, and he gets nailed for sending taunting e-mails to Clay Arnold. Wallace had suffered many indignities during his life, but he was stunned to his core with where he found himself now . . . jail.

Several minutes later, Rebecca Willett, Sheriff Hatfield, and Clarabelle arrived at the Putnam County jail and went into an observation room adjacent to Wallace's holding unit. They observed him through a two-way mirror. Wallace appeared to have shut down emotionally. He sat with his head bent and his eyes closed. He wore shackles on his ankles that were secured to the floor. Occasionally he rocked a little and whimpered. It saddened Clarabelle deeply to see her work friend in such an awful situation.

"Can we go see him?" Clarabelle asked Rebecca.

"Yeah, we can go see him," Rebecca replied. "I'm hoping he opens up to you. We've got to find Laura soon, and if he knows anything that helps us get her back safely, it may improve his case."

"I understand, Officer Willett."

The two women exited the observation room, and walked next door. Wallace did not raise his head as they entered. It was as if he was in a seated fetal position. Rebecca motioned for Clarabelle to approach him. She slowly stepped forward and then knelt down so she was on eye level with Wallace. Still, his eyes remained shut and his demeanor unresponsive.

"Wallace," she said softly. "Wallace, it's me, Clarabelle."

Wallace stirred at the sound of her voice and the mention of her name.

"Clarabelle?!" he asked, and his eyes fluttered open. "Oh, Clarabelle, I don't want you to see me like this. I'm just a chained-up worthless mess of a man." Tears formed in his eyes.

"Wallace, I'm here with Officer Willett. We want to help you, but we need to ask you some important questions. Will you please talk with us?"

"I'm so confused," Wallace said, "and these chains are hurting my ankles."

As a show of good faith, and because Rebecca had no doubt in her mind that she could physically subdue Mr. Bane if necessary, she unlocked his shackles. Rebecca motioned for the three of them to sit at a small table where they would be in plain view of Sheriff Hatfield and the officers seated behind the observation mirror.

"Mr. Bane, my name is Rebecca Willett, and I'm a detective with the Indiana State Police." She read him his Miranda rights again which he said he understood. Rebecca continued, "Mr. Bane, you don't need to answer any of my questions without the benefit of legal counsel, but a young girl has been abducted, and we are very concerned about her safety. Can you please help us? Are you the person responsible for her being missing, and do you know where she is?"

Wallace looked at Clarabelle whose eyes were imploring him to tell what he knew. Then he turned to Detective Willett and said, with all of the sincerity he could muster, "I swear I did not abduct that girl, and I don't know where she is."

Rebecca looked at him closely trying to determine if he was, in fact, telling the truth. At the police academy she had been trained to detect "tells" from a person's body language and facial expressions. She was surprised by how genuinely Wallace was coming across.

"What about the locked storeroom with the chains attached to the walls? Our forensics guys say that they were very recently hammered in place."

Wallace felt his world beginning to crumble again. He would not make eye contact with Clarabelle. "Yes, I put those chains there. I was going to somehow detain Clay Arnold's girlfriend, Maggie Bodine, but I failed."

"Why would you want to do something like that?" Clarabelle asked.

Still, Wallace would not look directly at Clarabelle. He was too ashamed. "I, I was hurt and jealous because Clay Arnold was receiving so much attention with his beautiful night sky photographs, and then he got an honorary doctorate from my own college, and all I have is a master's degree. Everyone gets to be called doctor except Wallace-the-Mole-Bane. So, I wanted to show everyone I was capable of pulling something like this off. I never intended to hurt Ms. Bodine, just embarrass Clay Arnold."

Wallace finally turned to face Clarabelle and said, "I know how pathetic this sounds, and I know I'm in a lot of trouble. I just want you to know that I have appreciated your being my friend."

"Of course, I'm your friend, Wallace. I wish maybe you had confided some of these feelings with me before all of this happened. I like you."

Wallace sat up in his chair. No one, especially a female, had ever uttered those words to him before.

"Wallace, we need to find the girl," Rebecca said. "And what's the story with the taunting e-mails to Clay and the mythological astronomy references?"

"Detective Willett, I swear I don't know anything about the e-mails. Perhaps if I saw them, I might be able to help put some pieces together."

Rebecca phoned Chief Hatfield and asked him to bring a printed copy of the e-mails that Mr. Bane purportedly sent to Clay Arnold. They were delivered a few minutes later.

"Mr. Bane," Rebecca began. "I want to reiterate that you are the prime suspect in this case, and if you are trying to lead us down a blind alley on this search, we have a cell down the hall where you can think about it for a long time. On the other hand, Mr. Bane, if you think you can uncover something tangible that results in Laura's recovery, the court may look favorably on your assistance."

Wallace gulped audibly. He turned his gaze toward Clarabelle and saw her give him an encouraging smile. "I understand," Wallace said evenly. "I admit that I have done some things that I shouldn't have, but I did not abduct Laura, and I never sent any e-mails to Clay Arnold. I want to help if I can."

Rebecca set the printed copies of the e-mails in front of Wallace and told him to review each carefully. The first thing that struck Wallace was clearly seeing his name as the sender on each one. Now he understood why the police were so quick in deciding upon his apprehension.

"This doesn't look good for me," Wallace said softly. "Not good at all."

He continued to review the e-mails, and he noticed how taunting and belittling the sender was to Clay Arnold.

"Whoever sent this sure is a pissy cuss!" Wallace blurted out and then apologized for his use of foul language. "It's the mythological references in the constellations that fascinate me. He sure has a savior fixation with Perseus and Princess Andromeda."

Rebecca watched Wallace's face very carefully as he reviewed the e-mails time and again. What she saw was someone hard at work trying to glean helpful information rather than a criminal who had just kidnapped a teenage girl. She was beginning to believe that he was not the abductor.

"It's clear that the sender is an individual who knows the constellations and ancient Greek mythology very well. In this day and age there are many knowledgeable amateur astronomers, citizen scientists if you will, who know about Cassiopeia, Andromeda, Perseus, and Pegasus. So, I'm not sure how that narrows the field of suspects, but those are my immediate reactions: Pissy cuss. Enjoys belittling. Knows astronomy."

And then it dawned on Wallace, and he turned to look at Clarabelle. Their eyes met with the dawning knowledge of who the perpetrator is. Almost in unison they declared, "Dr. Chestnut!" The cad!

"So, that's why he said he was going on vacation at the conclusion of the ceremony and reception!" Clarabelle said. "He's got Laura! It's not Wallace you want, Detective Willett, it's Dr. Mortimer Chestnut."

Rebecca immediately got on the phone to Sheriff Hatfield to come up with every bit of information he could on Mortimer Chestnut, especially credit card details and properties owned. President Murray was immediately contacted as well, and he subsequently instructed the college's human resources department and campus security to provide law enforcement with everything they had on Dr. Chestnut. Finding the location of Mortimer's home in town took only a few minutes, and three squad cars were immediately dispatched to that location.

Before instructing his men to approach the home, Sheriff Hatfield first telephoned the residence to see if anyone was there. No one answered. Sheriff Hatfield gave the word, and his men surrounded the house. When everyone was in place, two officers simultaneously burst through the front and rear doors. Four other officers joined them, and they cleared the house one room at a time. They paid particular attention to the basement and the attic. No one was home, and nothing looked unusual. An occasional police radio squawked, but it was otherwise quiet. The officers found nothing suspicious at Dr. Chestnut's home, and they informed the command center. They exited the home, leaving one officer to guard the house and attached yellow crime scene tape to the remains of the doors.

Chapter 22

MAGGIE AND CLAY LEFT the observatory and returned to the Walden Inn to await Maggie's sister and her husband's arrival. Rita and Tom had managed to charter a small corporate jet that brought them directly to Putnam County airport. From there they were picked up by Sheriff Hatfield who had left the jail to personally bring them to the Inn.

Once everyone was inside Sheriff Hatfield gave them a status report on their search and investigation. "Here's where we stand at this point. We have apprehended a suspect and questioned him thoroughly, and while there is evidence implicating that person, we are beginning to believe that

the perpetrator is actually someone different. We have already been to that new suspect's home and searched it thoroughly. Unfortunately, the search revealed nothing helpful."

"So, who is this new suspect?" Tom asked.

"The dean of the astronomy department at the college," Sheriff Hatfield reported. "A chap named Dr. Mortimer Chestnut."

"You're kidding!" Clay said. "President Murray introduced me to him shortly before the ceremony."

"Well, Dr. Chestnut apparently decided to take a vacation at the conclusion of the reception, and no one knows where he is at this point," Hatfield said. "We're turning over every stone, but he and Laura could be anywhere now."

"That certainly doesn't sound very encouraging, sheriff," Tom said with frustration in his voice.

"I understand your annoyance, sir," the sheriff replied. "I would probably feel the same way if I were in your shoes, but I can assure you that local police departments are working in concert with the Indiana State Police, and we're not going to rest until we get Laura back safely."

"Tom and Rita," Clay said, "we know how frightening this situation is. There's not much that any of us can do right now except let law enforcement follow any leads they uncover. May I suggest that Maggie take you back to my home near Indy, and that you stay there until we know something more definitively."

Sheriff Hatfield nodded his agreement and said, "I promise you we will notify you of any developments as they occur."

Rita looked at Maggie as if to ask what her sister thought. Maggie agreed that it made sense, and I gave her the keys to my truck and the GPS coordinates to the brewery complex. While the Inn's staff helped Tom and Rita move their luggage from the lobby to Clay's Tacoma, Maggie stayed in the room with Clay.

"I am so scared," Maggie said to Clay. "And it hurts me so to see my sister so frightened as well. I know there are violent sides to you that I have never seen and really never wish to see, but I'm begging you to do whatever it takes to help get my niece back safely . . . anything!" Tears formed in Maggie's eyes again.

I pulled Maggie close and held her. "We'll get her back safely," I promised even though I had no clue how we were going to accomplish that. "I'll text Tori, Weed, and Mace to let them know you're all coming. We'll get through this," I promised again as I lightly stroked Maggie's hair. I walked her outside the Inn to join Rita and Tom at my Tacoma. They all got settled and departed a few minutes later.

Try as I might to control it, my blood was beginning to boil with anger. I had managed to keep my dark side under control while I was with Maggie, but now my desire to get Laura back and even the score with this pompous scumbag Chestnut was starting to take over. I rooted around in my camera bag until I found what I was looking for. The Demon camera was where I had concealed it. I checked its battery and saw that it was fully charged. I slipped it in my jacket pocket and left the room to meet Sheriff Hatfield. We drove to the jail to join Rebecca Willett, and to see what else Wallace Bane had been able to glean from the e-mails. One thing I believed for sure, time was potentially running out on finding Laura.

Laura lay on the cot in the locked room. There were no windows, and her only source of illumination was a bare lightbulb overhead. There was an ancient looking sink, a stained toilet, and her cot. She gave up trying to get the man whose voice she had heard earlier to come back. She gave up screaming and pleading. She had no more tears to shed. Laura was alone, and she listened intently to the quiet. And in this quiet she tried to resurrect what happened at the observatory. She remembered going behind the refreshment area to help that professor with a surprise for Clay, and then everything went blank.

She remembered feeling a very odd stiffness in her muscles when she woke up and a funny taste in her mouth. And, she remembered the man's voice. It was that creepy professor's voice. And then, of course, there was the Why. Why would he want to kidnap her and hold her against her will?

Mortimer Chestnut sat at his makeshift desk at the kitchen table. From here he could also see partway down his lane to the county road. He made certain that his perimeter security system was operating properly including his outside surveillance cameras. He doubted that the police would ever find his hidden cabin, but he wanted to be sure he could see them coming, just in case.

"Hmmm, perhaps it's time to send another message to my good pal, Clay Arnold," Mortimer mused. He reviewed his list of annoying e-mails he had prepared in advance for the new Doctor Arnold, and he hit "Send". "It's so sad that my underling, Wallace Bane, will get the blame for this," he chuckled out loud to himself. "Wallace Bane, what a loser. He deserves being called the Mole. When I'm finally president of Kissinger College, that feebleminded dweeb will get the boot, and Ms. Meemo may just have to suffer the same fate!"

From below Mortimer heard pounding on the cellar door and the faintly muffled cries of his incarcerated guest. "Perhaps the little dear is hungry,"

Mortimer said aloud. "Sure wouldn't want her to starve to death before I can become a hero by saving her in the eyes of the authorities and implicating poor Wallace. A couple more hours of driving the police nuts before I swoop in like mighty Perseus and save sweet little Andromeda from perishing. Then, it'll be a matter of time before the college's trustees deem my heroism as ample reason to boot that old coot Murray and install me to the position of leadership that I've longed for."

Sheriff Hatfield and I arrived at the jail and joined Rebecca, Clarabelle, and Wallace in the secure room where Wallace was being held. Lacking any new evidence, Wallace was still viewed as a suspect in Laura's abduction even though he was cooperating with the authorities. A ding sounded on Clay's phone just as he sat next to Rebecca Willett. They immediately viewed the message which was supposedly sent by Mr. Bane. The only problem was that Mr. Bane was sitting right next to them.

"Ah Doctor Arnold," the message began, *"it is so sad that you haven't been able to rescue poor Andromeda. She's so hungry and alone and cries pitifully. Perhaps a smarter person may prove to be her heroic Perseus."*

"Well, perhaps it's time that we ended this charade and finally responded to this arrogant jerk,"

Rebecca suggested. She forwarded the message on to her boss, Trent Reynolds, and to the tech staff at the Indiana State Police. Clay nodded his agreement and privately breathed a sigh of relief that Maggie and sister and brother-in-law were not present to see the frightening e-mail about Laura.

Rebecca composed the following message and showed it to Sheriff Hatfield and Clay: *"Give it up, Dr. Chestnut. We know that you are the culprit who abducted Laura, not Wallace Bane, and we're coming for you. You're finished!"*

"This message should shake things up a bit," I said and pressed the send button.

A few nanoseconds later, a new message appeared on the computer screen Mortimer was viewing, and he screamed in outrage. "How dare they!" he sputtered. "How dare they discover that it's me and not Wallace the Mole!"

He kicked his chair out of the way and headed for the door leading downstairs to his captive's cell. "Well, we'll just see about this!" he bellowed, and for the first time Dr. Chestnut saw his likely ascension to the president's office beginning to slip irretrievably away. "Perhaps, sweet little Andromeda won't get to be saved after all," he fumed, and he strode angrily down the steps to take his frustrations out on his captive.

Chapter 23

F OR THE FIRST TIME SINCE he had been detained
by the police, Wallace Bane breathed a sigh of
relief. He looked at Clarabelle who was sitting next
to him, and she gave his hand a small squeeze of
encouragement. Rebecca and the local police were
not ready to release him yet, and Rebecca and Sheriff
Hatfield telephoned Trent at ISP headquarters to let
him know they were now focusing on Dr. Mortimer
Chestnut as the kidnapper instead of Wallace Bane.

"So, how do you plan on capturing this guy?"
Trent asked Rebecca on the phone.

"Well. sir, we have a real-time watch on his
credit cards in place, but he hasn't charged anything

yet which leads us to surmise that he has another property nearby, maybe still in Putnam County, where he's holed up with the girl."

"Sounds reasonable," Trent said, "but he's a clever fellow, and he could be anywhere by now. Keep me informed, okay?"

Clarabelle and Wallace listened intently to their conversation, and when Rebecca and Trent hung up, Clarabelle offered, "Perhaps if Wallace and I looked at the county's property records, we might be able to come up with something."

Rebecca and Sheriff Hatfield had already directed their staff to find another property owned by Mortimer Chestnut in addition to his home on Seminary Street, but nothing substantive had been found. They were stymied.

"Have at it," Sheriff Hatfield encouraged, and he placed the county's property records in front of them. Clarabelle and Wallace saw the huge tome that the chief placed on the table and gulped. Even though Putnam County only had a population of some 37,000, there were a ton of property transactions over the past eight years which pretty much coincided with the length of time Mortimer Chestnut had been employed at the college. Anticipating a long night, Sheriff Hatfield requested that dinner and beverages be brought in. What was originally Wallace Bane's holding room now became their command center, and Clarabelle and Wallace methodically dove into the real estate records hoping to discover any leads at all.

I stood idly by watching a flurry of activity by the police which amounted to little more than a lot of sound and fury indicating nothing. I called Maggie to give her and Tom and Rita an update which entailed very little new information other than telling them that we had confronted Dr. Mortimer Chestnut with the knowledge that we knew he was the culprit.

After Maggie and I spoke, I called and talked briefly with Weed and told him where we stood and asked him to try to make our new guests' stay at the brewery as comfortable as possible.

Wallace and Clarabelle had already gone through the As, Bs, and Cs alphabetically and were starting to hit their stride in scanning through the records. Even at that, I was concerned by how long it might take for them to get through the pages of listings. Not surprising, they found nothing in the Cs aside from Dr. Chestnut's listing on Seminary Street which the police had already cleared.

Mortimer Chestnut descended the steps into the basement and approached the locked door. He could hear Laura weeping on the other side. He set aside the bowl of food he brought for her as he unlocked the heavy door. He stepped inside and saw his hostage sitting on the side of her cot.

"There, there, Princess Andromeda, I brought you some food," he said mockingly. "Now, if you're a very good girl, you may get to leave here someday."

"Someday!" she erupted. "Why have you kidnapped me? I want to go home now, you creep, and my name is Laura, not Andromeda!"

Mortimer was taken aback by her rude directness. He laid the bowl of food on the floor and told her to behave herself. "I would craft my words a little more carefully if I were you, young lady. My plans have just been turned upside down, and your snippiness isn't helping matters any. Do try to be a little more ladylike."

Laura responded by leaping to a standing position and launching a foot in the direction of Mortimer's head. He felt a swoosh of air as it just missed its mark.

"How's that for ladylike, you creepy jerk!" she verbally hurled at him. "Let me go now!"

Being the coward that he was, Mortimer receded to the doorway just as another kick was directed at his groin. He quickly stepped outside and slammed the door shut. He heard Laura pound on the door with a few creative expletives thrown in for effect.

"Sheesh!" Mortimer said to himself. "These kids today just don't care about respecting their elders!" He returned to the stairway and walked back upstairs to the safety of his cabin. He sat in front of his computer monitor and thought about his next steps now that he'd been discovered by the police. Things weren't going quite as he'd expected and that meant a total change of plans. He thought for a few moments and then composed a fresh e-mail.

"Dear Doctor Arnold, and I use the title 'Doctor' with reservations, there has been a slight change of plans since you and the police now know my true identity. Please tell Wallace I hope there are no hard feelings for my dumping the blame for Laura's abduction on him. He was just such an easy, defenseless target. Now then, let's say that the price of dear Laura's freedom just went from essentially zero to $3 million, enough to keep me in a decent lifestyle since I seriously doubt that I'll be getting a salary from Kissinger College anymore. Oh, and do stay tuned for further instructions about the money!" He hit "Send".

Everyone in the command center straightened up when they heard the vibration coming from the inbox on my phone. Rebecca and Sheriff Hatfield looked over my shoulders as I read the distressing message.

"Well, it appears that we have a classic kidnapping case now with a ransom demand," Rebecca said, and she forwarded the message to Trent Reynolds at

ISP headquarters to let him know the latest development. Sheriff Hatfield nodded his head in agreement and said, "This ramps up the danger level a lot more, too. Chestnut is now growing desperate, and desperate people often do unpredictable, awful things. We need to make more progress and fast."

Clarabelle and Wallace looked up briefly from the county property book and then redirected their search with even greater urgency. They had made it though the Ms alphabetically but had nothing to show for their efforts.

"I don't know what else we can do, Wallace, except keep looking through these property records. I had hoped we'd find Chestnut's name under the Cs, but if it were that easy, I'm sure the police would've found it by now."

"Let's just keep looking, Clarabelle," Wallace urged. "We need to get Laura back soon before Mortimer goes further off the deep end, and maybe if we can help locate our boss and get Laura back safely, the authorities will go a little easier on me."

I needed a break from the frustrating tedium of waiting to hear back from Mortimer Chestnut. I had little doubt that the police were doing everything they could to find him, but not knowing what was coming next was starting to get under my skin.

I walked outside the building trying to practice patience and to get my growing rage to subside.

I shook my head in disbelief at the events of the past day. The highlights were meeting Wade Henry and his family, and, of course, receiving the honorary doctorate. I also viewed my conversations with Maggie as a major highlight. She was aware of my life as an avenging vigilante and hadn't thrown me away . . . yet. Moreover, from her begging me to do whatever it took to save Laura, I knew that she understood that desperate times often call for desperate measures.

The lowlights of the past day, of course, were Laura's abduction and the pain it was causing her family. Another lowlight was realizing how much two people, Mortimer Chestnut and Wallace Bane, hated my getting the recognition they thought they deserved. I knew I didn't do anything wrong to deserve their vitriol, but it cast a pall on what should've been a wonderful experience.

I closed my eyes and pictured Maggie's lovely face. My rage subsided. Feeling a little calmer, I returned inside to await whatever would come next.

Chapter 24

THE NEXT FEW HOURS came at a snail's pace. Officers were deployed all throughout Putnam County, but each scheduled call into the command center brought the same frustrating report: "Nothing here, sir."

I looked over at Rebecca, and she was leaning over the work table peering at the property records with Clarabelle and Wallace. Each of them was glued to the records, but as each letter of the alphabet came and went, a sense of futility was beginning to creep in.

"Well, we've made it to the Ss," Clarabelle said with an air of feigned enthusiasm. "There's a lot of

names that begin with S so I'm hopeful we'll finally find something."

"Let's keep at it," Rebecca said. "We can do this."

Clay admired Rebecca's positive professionalism and easily understood why Trent Reynolds was such a strong advocate for his junior officer. He went over to watch them reviewing the records.

Wallace Bane looked up and his eyes met mine, and he looked away in shame. "I'm so sorry, Dr. Arnold, I never really meant you or Ms. Bodine any harm. I, I got lonely and scared, and I let pettiness consume me. You are such a magnificent photographer, and I'm so embarrassed and ashamed of my behavior to you." Wallace hung his head.

For a very brief second I actually smiled to myself. Time was, I would've unapologetically eliminated anyone who threatened me and especially Maggie. I looked down at Wallace and felt not so much pity for him, but self-compassion for myself. It was an epiphany that I felt calmer and steadier in my willingness to forgive Wallace's transgressions.

"First of all, Mr. Bane, call me Clay. I think we have far too many people hung up on the doctor title around here, so why don't we just call each other by our first names, okay? And second, you're an excellent photographer in your own right. I've seen your night sky photographs published in *Space and*

Beyond magazine, and I'm aware they awarded you a very respectable honorable mention this year."

Wallace was stunned by Clay's words. He slowly looked up and met his gaze. "I don't know quite what to say, Clay. You honor me with your positive words about my night pictures. They're so important to me. And, your kindness is not something that I am accustomed to. I'm in your debt."

"Let's do this, Wallace," I said. "You come up with where Chestnut is holding Laura, and we get her back safely, your debt will be wiped clean as far as I'm concerned." I looked over at Rebecca, and she shrugged okay. "Let's get back to work," she said. "We can talk about this after we get Laura back."

It had already been a long day that was now stretching into night. Everyone knew that darkness wouldn't make our search any easier. I missed Maggie, and I walked outside again to give her a call. I felt badly that I had nothing substantive to report again, but I wanted to hear her voice.

"Hey there!" I said when she answered. "Just want to see how you guys are doing over there? I sure miss you, Maggie."

"We're doing about as well as can be expected under the circumstances," Maggie replied. "Actually, Weed and Tori and Rennie have kept us well-fed and even a little entertained. Rennie is so sweet. He told Rita and Tom he was really sorry he didn't keep a closer eye on Laura when he went to get their lemonade. That young man is a gem, Clay. And Tori and Weed have sung some songs for us, and along with Mace, they've basically embraced all of us into your family. So, yeah, we're doing okay, I guess. It's the not-knowing that is so difficult. Any more news?"

"No, nothing yet." I admitted. "I know it's very frightening. I just want you to know that we'll get through this. I promise." We hung up a few moments later.

It was now dark outside, and in spite of the lights in the parking lot, I could make out the details of a starry sky. I looked northeast and saw the constellations, Cassiopeia, and then Andromeda and Perseus and Pegasus. They had each maintained their stellar positions in the night sky for millennia since the ancient Greek and Roman poets wrote of their tales. And like the people of those faraway days, I gazed into the expanse above me and wondered what it was all about. It was growing late, and I was anxious for us to make some progress, any progress. I returned inside to join Rebecca, Wallace, and Clarabelle.

"We're into the Ts," Clarabelle said as I approached their work table. Wallace's eyes were glued to the property records, and he didn't bother to look up. I spoke with Sheriff Hatfield and Rebecca and asked if they had any other search plans at this point. He shared a couple of ideas about moving some of their officers to different positions with special emphasis on money machines, fast-food places, and gas stations. I knew they were all working hard, but we still weren't getting anywhere.

Clarabelle sat next to Wallace. They had both been working very hard looking through the property records, but she knew that Wallace was virtually consumed with the task at hand. She worried he was reaching the point of exhaustion.

"Tanner, Taylor, Templeton," Wallace read out loud. "Terrill, Tesmer, Thomas, Thompson," he murmured. And then he stopped speaking and just stared at the book. He saw a name that sent his senses on high alert, "Tip-top Properties". Could it be? Could Mortimer Chestnut have actually named this property after one of his favorite expressions . . .Tip-top? Clarabelle looked at Wallace who appeared to be in shock and asked if he was okay.

"That's it!" Wallace announced. I think I found it . . . Tip-top Properties!" At the mention of Chestnut's favorite word, Clarabelle looked at the record book, and shouted out loud, "Wallace found the property, and here's the location!"

Sheriff Hatfield, Rebecca, and I sprang toward the table to see what Wallace had discovered: Tip-top Properties located on County Road 250 N. near the Wurster Tree Farm. They were only eight miles away. The command center sprang into action, and Sheriff Hatfield and Rebecca Willett began implementing their rescue plan.

"Okay, listen up, people," Sheriff Hatfield said. "We've got to be smart about this. I've instructed my officers to collapse their search perimeter to a mile in any direction of 4235 W. County Road 250 N. That includes County Roads 190 and 400 and Brick Chapel Road. And no one, and I repeat no one is to move on that location without my personal order. We want to maintain a secure net around that location, and Detective Willett and I will lead a team of officers to approach the home listed as Tip-top Properties. Is that clear to everyone? Now then, let me know when you have moved to your new locations and stay alert for further communications from me. We've got one good shot at getting the girl back, and I don't want any screw-ups."

Three minutes later the command center began receiving reports from officers indicating that they were in their new positions. Rebecca contacted Trent at ISP headquarters in Indy who immediately dispatched a team of Indiana state troopers to secure an additional perimeter along State Route 231 in case Mortimer Chestnut got past the county sheriff's men.

I called Maggie to finally give her some good news to share with Rita and Tom and my friends at our brewery complex. "I can't talk long, Maggie, because we're getting ready to roll. Please tell Rita and Tom we'll do everything possible to try to keep Laura out of harm's way. I'll let you know the minute we have further news to report."

We spoke for just another few seconds and then hung up. I caught up to Rebecca and Sheriff Hatfield just as they were climbing into an unmarked police vehicle, and we sprayed a cyclone of gravel as we sped out of the parking lot.

"Let's go get us a bad guy and save the girl!" Sheriff Hatfield declared, and Rebecca and I tightened our seat belts.

Chapter 25

MORTIMER CHESTNUT SAT wearily at his makeshift desk in his secluded cabin. Laura's screaming from the locked room below him had ceased, and the cabin grew silent as the darkness of night enveloped them. It had been a long day, and not much had gone according to Mortimer's original plan to abduct Maggie Bodine, but he became dreamy-eyed thinking of the prospect of getting $3 million in ransom money for Laura's release.

"Screw the president's job! Now I need to craft a tip-top plan to get the dough without getting caught," Mortimer said aloud, and a germ of an idea came to him. "You can do this, Mortie my

boy. No cops could ever be smarter than you!" A few minutes later, his eyes began to droop, and Dr. Mortimer Chestnut finally succumbed to the seduction of sleep.

Sheriff Hatfield guided his cruiser onto State Route 231 and zoomed past the Greencastle police department on his way north. He had two more unmarked vehicles containing six officers following closely behind him. Traffic was light at this hour, and he made certain none of the police cars had their emergency sirens or lights in use. The small caravan of cruisers sped past the Putnam County Fairgrounds and up Waterworks Hill. They continued north for another two miles until they saw the white wooden sign for the Wurster Tree Farm. They turned west and cautiously crept along County Road 200 for another mile or so until they came to County Road 250 N. They were now about a mile from their destination.

I sat in the backseat of the cruiser behind Rebecca and Sheriff Hatfield and felt the tension grow as we proceeded toward Mortimer Chestnut's location. When we were within one hundred yards of the lane leading to Mortimer's cabin, Sheriff Hatfield pulled over to the side of the road, stopped, and killed his headlights. The other two cruisers followed his lead and awaited further instructions.

Rebecca, Sheriff Hatfield, and I got out of the car and reviewed the Google Maps image of Tip-top Properties on the Sheriff's mobile device. It showed a single structure surrounded by trees with a pond at the rear of the property. Sheriff Hatfield instructed his men in the other two cruisers to fan out through the trees and surround the cabin. We waited a full five minutes to give them time to get situated.

"It's your call, Sheriff," Rebecca said. "How do you want to proceed?"

"We know that Dr. Chestnut is a smart fellow," Hatfield said. "We also know that he has the advantage of holding a hostage, plus he knows the terrain. I'm guessing that the last thing he might suspect is a woman approaching his cabin. I think if Clay and I flank his front door from the trees, and you walk down the lane, he might not suspect anything too threatening. But that's pretty risky, too considering he knows that we're on to him. It's your decision, Rebecca. I'd prefer not to try a full-blown attack if that puts Laura in harm's way. If he bolts out the cabin's back door, my men will pick him up."

Rebecca thought about his suggestion a moment and said, "I'm game, Sheriff. Let me get rid of my official-looking gear, and I'll tuck my service revolver in the rear of my waistband."

Sheriff Hatfield quietly radioed his men to let them know that Detective Willett would be approaching the cabin on foot, and to stay alert in case Chestnut tries to flee. The Sheriff and I split up to positions just inside the tree line with a view of the cabin's front door. When we were in place, the Sheriff signaled Rebecca, and she began a casual stroll forward in the lane. The cabin ahead was dark without a sign of life.

Mortimer Chestnut had fallen into a deep sleep, and he dreamed of being a wealthy man without a care in the world. Even in his dream, he sensed his once-important career as an astronomy professor was over. He didn't care. His dream was that soothing, that promising. But his reverie was short-lived when all of a sudden the bells and whistles of his perimeter security system were tripped, and he damn near fell out of his chair. "What the . . .?!" he stammered. He looked at his computer monitor and saw a solitary woman approaching his cabin on foot. "Now what?!" he said to himself. He reached for his stun gun and quietly approached his front door. He waited and wondered if this was a neighbor, a lost motorist, or the law. He decided to remain anonymous, at least for the time being.

Rebecca approached the front porch of the cabin and called out, "Hello, anybody home? My car broke down on the road, and I could use a little help. Hello, anybody!"

Mortimer considered the likelihood of her lament but remained concealed.

Rebecca stepped on to the porch and approached the front door. She had no idea what to expect, and it was only her professional training and sheer guts that allowed her to proceed. She knocked on the door and again called out for assistance. Again, no reply. Now what?!

Mortimer felt a bit flummoxed about what he should do. He really didn't want to open the door. On the other hand, he didn't want some stranger wandering around his property. He decided to take a chance, and he opened the front door a crack. He had his stun gun hidden but at the ready.

"What do you want?" Mortimer asked with irritation in his voice. "I live in the woods because I don't like being bothered."

"Oh, I'm sorry, sir," Rebecca replied cheerfully. "I'm Kristi Phillips," Rebecca fibbed. I live down the road a ways and my car broke down. I don't have a phone with me, and I was hoping to maybe use yours to call my husband for a ride."

"Like I said," Mortimer replied, "I don't like being bothered. I can loan you my cell phone for a quick call, but you have to stay on the porch."

Clearly, Dr. Chestnut did not recognize Detective Willett from the ceremony earlier in the day, but she definitely recognized him from the photos the college's human resources staff had given to law enforcement. She breathed a sigh of relief that they had, indeed, located their man.

"That's fine, sir, and again I'm really sorry to bother you. My husband, Ralph, and I like living in the country for the same reason. Your lane was the closest to me, and honestly I didn't know where else I could go at this hour. I promise I'll be real fast."

Mortimer tossed her his cell phone through the partially opened front door and waited for her to make her call. And then he noticed her sturdy, polished black shoes and something in his mind screamed "cop". He pushed the door the rest of the way open and immediately zapped Rebecca with a full charge from his stun gun. She had no opportunity to react and fell to the porch floor in a twitching heap. Mortimer saw the service revolver hidden inside of her waistband, and he quickly grabbed it, along with his cell phone, and slammed the front door.

"Well, so much for the element of surprise," I said out loud to myself.

The Sheriff radioed his men who were guarding the perimeter to the cabin and told them about Detective Willett. He instructed them to maintain their positions and await further orders. He called me on his phone and told me to stay put and out of sight.

"Well Clay, it looks like we've got a bit of a standoff," Sheriff Hatfield said. "Dr. Chestnut knows we're out here, and he knows he's got to come out at some point. My guess is he's gonna want to wait it out a bit and then try to parlay the girl's release for his safe passage out of here."

I couldn't argue with the sheriff's reasoning, but I wasn't much in the mood for just sitting around waiting for Dr. Mortimer Chestnut to make the next move. My blood was beginning to boil again. Then, I saw Rebecca struggling to regain herself, and I did not like the thought of Chestnut cracking the door open and shooting her with her own handgun. I told Sheriff Hatfield, "I'm getting Rebecca." I took off running for the porch.

Adrenaline is an amazing thing. I tried not to think about Dr. Chestnut. I just wanted to get Rebecca out of the line of fire. The distance between us was only about twenty yards, most of which was protected from Mortimer's view. My worry was what he would do when he heard my feet hit the wooden porch. Like I said, adrenaline is an amazing chemical, and I tried not to think too much. I covered the twenty yards quickly and caught up to Rebecca just as she was trying to stand up. I reached around her waist and began leading her off the porch when I heard Mortimer's voice from the doorway. "You can keep her, but the girl's freedom is going to cost you three million dollars . . . and you better act fast because my patience doesn't last very long." The front door closed shut again.

I managed to lead Rebecca into the trees again and asked her if she was alright. She acknowledged that she was but needed to sit down again to recover more from the electrical shock. Sheriff Hatfield saw that I had safely recovered her, and he radioed his officers to let them know she was safe.

"That was a damn dumb thing you just did, Clay. You got lucky. From here on out, you follow my orders, okay?"

I replied, "okay," but I knew that my future compliance was based solely on the circumstances at the time. So now we were back to square one in our standoff with Mortimer Chestnut.

Just then my cell phone vibrated indicating a new message from Chestnut. His demands were succinct and to the point. "I need you to have a fully fueled helicopter land in the pasture across the county road from our location. I need you to have three million dollars in unmarked bills in the helicopter, and I need safe passage from my cabin to the helicopter. I am taking the girl with me and any attempt to rescue her will result in a most unfortunate accident occurring to her. Once I get to where I'm going, I will release the girl unharmed."

Clay showed the message to Rebecca who was slowly regaining her composure. With Rebecca's help composing a reply, I wrote back to Chestnut and copied the Sheriff and Trent Reynolds. "We are willing to comply with your demands, Chestnut, but it's going to take some time to collect the three million dollars and to get a helicopter to our location."

"Now, now, Dr. Arnold," Mortimer responded. "We both know that none of my demands are unreasonable. You've got one hour to have everything that I've requested in place, or really ugly things are going to happen to that lovely young girl." And to punctuate his seriousness, Mortimer fired Rebecca's service revolver into the air. "Get to it!" Mortimer wrote. "Or my next shot will have more lethal consequences."

Chapter 26

IT WASN'T LOST ON REBECCA or me that Dr. Mortimer Chestnut's behavior had gone from being that of a pedantic, taunting college professor to that of an angry, threatening fugitive. The euphoric prospect of his getting three million dollars, plus the intense stress of being surrounded by armed police had transformed Mortimer into a formidable adversary. He was cornered, but not yet desperate.

"I think our situation just got even more dangerous," Rebecca said. He's probably capable of taking a life now whereas before he probably never would've dreamed of it. We need to keep him thinking that we are doing everything possible to satisfy his demands."

I nodded my understanding. I was very worried about Laura, and even though I'm not a religious guy, I privately prayed that she was going to be safe. I thought about calling Maggie to give her an update, but given the tenuousness of the situation, I decided it was best to wait.

Rebecca had recovered sufficiently from the stun gun and was now on the phone with Trent Reynolds at ISP headquarters. Trent was making arrangements for the helicopter and the cash to be readied and deployed to the GPS coordinates in the open field near Mortimer's Tip-top Properties.

Rebecca informed Sheriff Hatfield about what Trent and the ISP were doing to meet Mortimer's demands, and she helped me prepare another e-mail to Chestnut.

The message read, "We have your three million dollars ready, and it's being flown by a single helicopter pilot to the location you indicated. It'll be here in the next thirty minutes. We will notify you when he has landed in the field and discuss your and Laura's transfer to that site."

"See, Dr. Arnold!" Mortimer replied. "All things are possible with a little creative ingenuity. I await your next communication. Don't disappoint me!"

"One other thing, Dr. Chestnut," I replied. "We're not doing anything further until you call me so I can hear Laura's voice. We need to make certain that the girl is okay. Here's my phone number."

Mortimer was not pleased by my demand, but called me and asked me to wait while he walked over to the door leading to the basement and descended the stairs to her "room." Laura heard him approaching and immediately began hollering and banging on the locked door. Mortimer and I immediately heard the ruckus that Laura was creating.

"You hear that racket, Dr. Arnold? That's your little darling. I'm not opening her door until we're ready to leave, so you'll just have to satisfy yourself that she is healthy enough to cause this cacophony." Chestnut held the phone to the door for me to hear more. I was satisfied it sounded like Laura.

"Look Mortimer," I said. "There's no reason to harm the girl. I'm the person you're angry with anyway. Why don't we swap me for the girl. You've got a gun, and I'll be unarmed. I'll do what you ask, so why don't we just make a trade . . . her for me?"

"Oh gee, what a nice offer," Mortimer replied sarcastically. "I don't think so, though. While I could shoot you if I needed to, young Laura will be much more manageable, especially if I zap her with the stun gun again." He hung up.

Over the next several minutes Sheriff Hatfield repositioned his men so they were covering the lane leading to the county road while still surrounding Chestnut's cabin. "Keep alert, men," he said. "He's a clever fella, and just because he says he's taking the helicopter out of here, doesn't mean that he won't try to throw us a curve and bolt out the rear door."

Rebecca and I walked through the trees to join Sheriff Hatfield and discuss next steps. "Looks like the only thing we can do now is wait for the helicopter to arrive," Sheriff Hatfield said.

"From my last conversation with Chestnut, it was obvious that Laura was secure in a locked room," I said. "It's possible we could just rush the cabin, and she would be safe."

Rebecca acknowledged that possibility. "On the other hand, Clay, we don't have a clue to what he's got boobytrapped inside, and the risk is too great."

"I guess you're right, Rebecca," I replied. "I'm just not accustomed to standing around waiting. There's nothing to lose by being patient for the helicopter to arrive."

The minutes dragged on and felt more like hours. Hatfield's men were in place, and Chestnut's cabin was dimly lit inside. More minutes passed, and then we heard the ever so distant hum of a helicopter's rotors. With each second that passed the drone grew louder, and we finally saw the copter's lights looming low over the horizon. Thirty seconds later, it landed in the field across the road.

I composed another message to Mortimer to let him know that everything he requested was in place.

"Now then," he responded. "I want you to have a car driven to my front door and left for me there with the engine running. The girl and I will drive the car to the field, get in the helicopter and leave. I'll let you know where you can find Laura when I get to my destination. Needless to say, any attempt to rescue her or to capture me will be met with a swift and unfortunate reaction."

Rebecca and I read his instructions and forwarded them on to Sheriff Hatfield and Trent Reynolds. The sheriff did as he was instructed and one of their unmarked police cruisers was driven down the lane and parked in front of Dr. Chestnut's cabin and left there with the engine running. The driver then joined the sheriff in the trees.

A few minutes later signs of activity could be seen at the cabin. "Step lively now," Mortimer instructed Laura. He had gone downstairs to her locked room and pointed his gun directly at her face. "We're going on a little adventure, Princess Andromeda, and your life expectancy will be dictated by how well you follow my instructions, and I mean to the letter. Is that understood, dearie?"

She nodded her understanding. "Where are we going?" she asked. "And quit calling me Andromeda, you pervert."

"Insults won't help your life expectancy much, either," Mortimer replied with menace in his voice. With the revolver trained on her, and his hand gripping Laura's arm, they walked up the basement steps and out on to the porch. He saw no officers, but from his surveillance equipment, he knew they were scattered around his cabin and down the lane to the road.

"Move!" he demanded to Laura. "Get in the passenger's seat and strap yourself in."

"Where are we going?!" Laura screamed at him. "I'm not going anywhere with you!" She tried to swat his hand off her arm but his grip tightened. "Get off of me!" Laura hurled at Mortimer.

"Be still, young lady, or I swear I will belt you!" Between having one hand on Laura's arm and his other hand holding the gun, he couldn't reach for the stun gun to subdue this hellcat he had on his hands now. He thought about smacking her head with the gun, but his professorial lifestyle had made him squeamish at the thought of blood.

"Be still!" Mortimer commanded again, but Laura would have none of his threats. She was one pissed-off kid!

I came out of the woods just as I saw fourteen-year-old Laura turn to face her captor and raise a ferocious knee into Mortimer's tender, unprotected groin. The expression on Dr. Chestnut's face was first one of recognition that he'd been kneed, and then the actual nauseating pain associated with crunched balls. Mortimer's eyes bugged out, and he was incapable of uttering anything other than a long baleful moan. His grip on Laura's arm immediately loosened, and she broke free and ran in the direction of my voice. I had her, and she was safe.

Dr. Chestnut had managed to regain enough wind to drag himself over to the waiting car. He leaped inside, slammed the door shut, and scattered a rooster-tail of gravel as he sped for the lane and the helicopter waiting in the field across the road. All the police officers ran from their positions to their waiting vehicles and launched a hasty pursuit. I left Laura in Rebecca's protection and leaped into Sheriff Hatfield's car.

But Mortimer didn't need to go far. He raced down his short lane and didn't even bother to look for traffic before launching his car airborne over County Road 250 N. and into the grassy field. He spied the helicopter and gunned his car toward it. If the situation weren't so serious, I could've found some humor in this chase. It looked like something out of the Keystone Cops. But it was serious. Mortimer slammed on his brakes as he approached the waiting helicopter. His groin was still sore from

Laura's parting salvo, but he ran for the helicopter. He peered inside to make certain the pilot wasn't armed and then awkwardly piled into the passenger seat with his gun trained on the pilot.

Sheriff Hatfield had his men position their vehicles in a circle about twenty-five feet from the helicopter. Their headlights lit up the scene like a movie set. Sheriff Hatfield parked our car next to the car Mortimer drove, and the sheriff and I got out and cautiously approached the helicopter.

"Get us out of here!" Mortimer shouted at the pilot. "Now, damn it!"

But the pilot looked over at him and said, "Let's end this now, Dr. Chestnut. You're surrounded, and I didn't bring you three million dollars. And even if you shoot me, you don't know how to fly a helicopter, do you?"

Mortimer looked at the pilot with a dawn of recognition that his reach for glory and riches had ended in a humiliating defeat.

Sheriff Hatfield and I approached Mortimer's door. I had my Demon camera in my hand just in case, and Sheriff Hatfield had his service revolver pointed at Mortimer's head. Mortimer kept his gun trained on the pilot, but his resolve was weakening.

I looked at the pilot and saw that it was none other than my good friend, Trent Reynolds, Assistant Superintendent of the Indiana State Police. I heard

Trent calmly say to him, "You're not a killer, Dr. Chestnut, please give me your gun and let's end this now before something really tragic happens."

Trent held his hand out to Mortimer. Mortimer's eyes danced to Trent, to Sheriff Hatfield, to me, and to the circle of police vehicles. He finally glanced down at Trent's open hand and placed the handgun he'd taken from Rebecca into it. Sheriff Hatfield immediately opened Mortimer's door and half-carried him out into the field. He turned him around and handcuffed his hands behind his back. I watched as the other officers joined the sheriff who searched Mortimer and read him his Miranda rights. They then deposited him into a cruiser containing three serious-looking officers. The chase was over. Laura was safe. The bad guy got caught, and I didn't have to kill anyone. All in all it was about as good as I could've hoped for.

Trent Reynolds got out of the pilot's seat and gave me a wink. "You didn't think I was going to let you get all of the action, did you, Clay?" Trent mused.

"You're something else, Trent. I didn't even know you could fly. You put yourself at a lot of risk coming for Chestnut."

"Yeah, well, goes with the job," Trent said. "Is Laura okay?"

"I think so," I replied. "I left her with Rebecca. You should know that your fine deputy took a full zap from Mortimer's stun gun about an hour ago. She's a brave officer, Trent."

"I know. Thanks for telling me, though, because I doubt that she would have."

Just then another police vehicle arrived on the scene, and Rebecca and Laura stepped out. Laura ran up to Clay and held on to him tightly.

Rebecca gave Trent a quick update on Laura's status. "She said Dr. Chestnut didn't physically harm her in any way, and aside from signs of fatigue and stress and some banged-up fists from pounding on her locked door, she seems okay."

"How about you?" Trent asked Rebecca. "Clay told me what Chestnut did to you."

"I'm alright. Not something I want to experience again, though," Rebecca admitted.

Sheriff Hatfield and his men cleared the field. One officer stayed behind at Mortimer's cabin, and the sheriff and the rest of his men escorted Dr. Mortimer Chestnut to the Putnam County jail.

Trent asked Rebecca, Laura, and me to get in the helicopter. "It'll be a little tight, but I think our weight limit is fine. Anyone have any objections to my flying us to a pretty courtyard I know at an old beer brewery along the White River?"

I couldn't think of anything I wanted more. The flight back to my home was relatively quiet. The droning sound of the rotors lulled us into a collective calm. Each of us had been tested and managed to come through. Laura rested her head on my shoulder and held Rebecca's hand. I called Maggie and gave her the good news. "We're coming home . . . all of us."

Chapter 27

IT WAS ALMOST MIDNIGHT by the time Trent guided the helicopter along the White River and saw the brewery complex. It would've been hard to miss. The entire place was lit up. Even from a distance I could easily make out Weed and Tori's farmhouse, Mace and Rennie's power plant, and my residence in the renovated brewhouse. Our brightly lit domiciles bordered the courtyard and marked a perfect landing area.

Trent turned on the helicopter's spotlight and put the aircraft down on the cobblestones with barely a bump. I could see everyone gathered on the front porch of the farmhouse, and once the copter's rotors

came to a complete stop, they all rushed to greet us. Laura was the first person out of the copter, and she flew into Tom and Rita's waiting arms. It was a very touching scene, one that I was very happy to witness given all of the dreadful things that could've happened during Mortimer Chestnut's frightening fall from reason.

Trent and Rebecca exited the copter next, and I was the last one out. Maggie was there waiting for me, and we held each other for a long several seconds.

"You did it!" she said as she buried her face into my neck. "You saved Laura."

"Thanks, sweetheart, but I had a lot of help, and Laura probably did more to save herself than any of us did. I'll tell you about it later."

Trent and Sheriff Hatfield communicated with their command centers and contacted President Murray to let him know that Dr. Chestnut had been apprehended and was setting up residence in the Putnam County jail awaiting formal charges of kidnapping, menacing, resisting arrest, Internet fraud, and a host of other charges that would guarantee his incarceration for a very long time.

Rita and Tom approached Maggie and me, and the look of appreciation in their eyes was heartwarming. They had their beautiful daughter back, relatively unharmed, and all was right with their world. Rennie, Weed, Tori, and Mace had held back from joining the throng until Laura had reunited with her parents, and now they surrounded all of us with hugs. It was wonderful finally being at home. Even Lex and Satchmo joined in, and Laura and Rennie finally laid eyes on each other for the first time since Rennie had gone to get them lemonade at the observatory.

"There you are!" Rennie declared when his eyes met Laura's. "Next time, I'm not letting you out of my sight!" he said.

Laura gave Rennie a huge hug, and said, "I'm sorry I scared you."

I introduced Trent to Rita and Tom and told them how Trent had thwarted Mortimer Chestnut's escape. Everyone was exhausted. It didn't seem possible that it was just earlier in the day that I had met Wade Henry and received an honorary doctorate from Kissinger College. It was a very bittersweet day, one that none of us was likely to ever forget. Given the hour, it was agreed that we'd all gather at the farmhouse for breakfast in the morning. Rebecca and Trent would be returning to their Indiana State Police headquarters yet that night to file reports and communicate further with the local police in Putnam County. Tom and Rita teared up when they said goodbye, and Laura approached Rebecca and gave her a long grateful hug. She struggled to find adequate words to express her appreciation, but each knew how life-altering their shared experiences had been.

Tori, Weed, Mace, and Rennie surrounded me and Maggie. Mace had a broad smile on his face, and he shook his head in amused amazement that I had managed to live through another potentially deadly experience. "You're like a cat with nine lives!" he remarked. "Make that more like eighteen lives!" Weed added.

"We all got lucky," I replied truthfully. "If Laura hadn't kneed Chestnut's nuts, and Trent hadn't foiled Mortimer's escape attempt, we could still be living in a nightmare."

We all parted company at that point. Laura and her parents would be staying in my guest rooms, and Maggie and I would be bunking in my bedroom in the floor above them. "Until breakfast then," I said, and Satchmo, our Maine Coon cat, fell in step with all of us heading for my place. A few moments later I heard the rotor from Trent's helicopter, and I thought about how fortunate I was to count him and Rebecca as trusted, reliable friends. We all had stuck together and survived.

Once inside my brew house, Maggie and I made certain that Tom, Rita, and Laura had everything they needed, and then we ascended the steps leading to my bedroom. We were both beyond exhaustion, and I planned on holding her close all night long.

"You did it, Clay," Maggie said. "You did everything you promised to do. You got Laura back safely, and yourself, too. I will never doubt or question you again. You're a hero, Dr. Arnold."

Instead of replying with words, I looked deeply into Maggie's green eyes, and the sense of relief that I felt brought tears to mine. "We all did the best we could," were the only words I could muster.

"I'm going to take a quick bath," Maggie said. "Then I don't want to ever let you go, Clay Arnold."

Maggie receded to the bathroom, and I walked out on to my roof garden to view the night sky with my devoted feline, Satchmo. I shook my head in disbelief when I thought about the events of the last day. Satchmo rubbed his huge flank against my leg and jumped up on the table next to where I was standing. I looked up into the night sky and spied familiar constellations. I doubted that I would ever be able to look upon Cassiopeia, Andromeda, and Perseus the same way after Mortimer Chestnut's twisted inclusion of their mythology into his plot.

A few minutes later Maggie came out of the bathroom wrapped in a soft bath towel. She looked stunning and serene, and I couldn't imagine not having her in my life. We both held each other, and

Satchmo did his best to make it a threesome. We stayed like that for several long moments.

"I didn't need to hurt anyone tonight," I said to Maggie. "Trent, Rebecca, and Laura did the most dangerous parts, and I, well I just wanted to find another way. There have been too many times over the past couple of years that I felt like a man on a ledge, and that my life could go one way or another as an avenging vigilante. With you in my life, Maggie, I feel like I have evened the score enough for those who are vulnerable. I want us to be together always and to find peace."

"That's how I feel, too, Clay, but you need to know that I trust you and your judgment implicitly, and I will not tell you how to live your life going forward."

We held each other closely for a few moments longer, and then Maggie led me inside toward the bedroom. Even in the dim light, I saw a flash of brilliance in her emerald eyes, "There's one more thing you need to know, Clay," she said with unbridled joy . . . "I'm pregnant!"

Chapter 28

A FEW DAYS LATER Clarabelle Meemo drove her Subaru Forester out of the parking lot next to the administration building on Kissinger College's main campus. She was on a special assignment from her uncle, President Hannibal Murray. The fall colors were a welcome sight, and she enjoyed seeing students walking on campus from one building to another. After experiencing a depraved episode like the one Mortimer Chestnut had foisted on everyone at the college, seeing the bright young faces on the students gave Clarabelle a sense of reassurance about the future of humanity.

Clarabelle drove down College Street past the Green Center for the Performing Arts and the Kurtzmann Science Center where her office in the astronomy department was located. She navigated her car around the old student union and continued north a few blocks until she came to Franklin Street. She turned east and continued until she came to DePauw Avenue and the Von Timm Observatory. It looked much different than it had a few days ago for the doctorate ceremony. There was no temporary stage or guest seating on the lawn. No canopy over a refreshment area. No Mortimer Chestnut making unreasonable demands of his staff. It was quiet, even serene looking.

Clarabelle parked her Forester in the circle around the observatory and got out. The front door was open, and she entered its fresh-looking lobby. No one was around. She had a feeling that Wallace would be working in his office in the basement, so she descended the steps one flight and saw his closed door. She quietly opened the door a bit and saw Wallace deep in thought over star charts he had laid out on his desk.

"Knock, knock!" she said, and Wallace darn near leaped out of his chair.

"Oops, sorry," she said with a laugh. "I didn't know I would spook you that much!"

"Oh Clarabelle, you gave me quite a start. I didn't hear you enter the observatory. I was just going over some charts. There's a fascinating occlusion occurring from a binary star rotating around Algol which is the beta star in the constellation Perseus."

Clarabelle smiled at Wallace. "You're the real star, Wallace. You shine brighter than you realize. If it hadn't been for you figuring out the Tip-top Properties location, Dr. Chestnut may have actually gotten away with his creepy plan with Laura. And, can you imagine him as president of Kissinger?" She shivered at the thought.

Wallace shivered as well. "I think I just got lucky," he said modestly.

Clarabelle walked over to him and took his hand. She then leaned forward and kissed him lightly on the cheek. "I'm very proud of you, Wallace." He blushed like a school boy. "But this isn't entirely a social call, Mr. Bane. President Murray has asked me to bring you to his office immediately. He said there is something very important that requires your personal presence."

"But I," Wallace stammered. "Have I done something wrong? Am I in trouble again? I don't know what it could possibly be!"

"I don't know, either, Wallace, but he said I was not to return without you. He was pretty firm about it."

Wallace folded up his star charts and put them in his print cabinet. He looked at himself in the mirror above his sink and asked Clarabelle if he looked presentable enough.

"You're just fine, Wallace," she reassured him. "C'mon, we don't want to keep the president waiting."

Together they straightened up a few things on Wallace's desk, and Clarabelle guided him toward the door and up the stairs to the observatory's lobby.

"I can't possibly imagine why the president would want to see me!" Wallace exclaimed. "Do you have a clue, Clarabelle?"

"Not really, Wallace, but he was very insistent on seeing you right away."

They got inside of Clarabelle's Forester, and she drove down DePauw Avenue heading back toward the administration building. She looked over at Wallace, and he looked petrified.

"Wallace, perhaps you might try to relax a bit. Whatever President Murray wants couldn't be as bad as you're making it out to be."

"Right," Wallace replied. "Try to relax."

Clarabelle gave his hand a gentle squeeze, and Wallace actually relaxed a little. "There you go," she said. "You'll be fine. I'm sure he's not mad at you."

Clarabelle pulled into the lot next to the administration building and parked in the same reserved spot she left thirty minutes earlier. Wallace was surprised by how full the lot looked at this hour. They got out, and Clarabelle gently took Wallace's arm. It was a very sweet gesture, plus she wanted to make sure that he didn't run for the hills. They entered the building and took the elevator to the third floor and walked into the foyer of President Murray's office.

"Please wait here, Wallace, I'll only be a moment," Clarabelle said, and she knocked, then stepped inside President Murray's office.

Wallace was alone with his thoughts. He looked around the warmly appointed foyer and appreciated its history and the influential people who had stood within it. In his own way, Wallace was truly devoted to Kissinger College. But he loved it from afar like an unwanted family member. Still, it was his family.

Clarabelle opened the door to the president's office and motioned for Wallace to enter. Once he was inside, she exited the office and closed the door leaving Wallace with his thoughts and the impressive presence of Dr. Hannibal Murray, President of Kissinger College.

President Murray stood up from his desk and walked across the room to welcome Wallace. "Mr. Bane, thank you very much for coming on such short notice. I know you are very busy at the observatory, and this tragic development with Dr. Chestnut has put a great deal of stress on everyone in the astronomy department. In some ways I envy you being removed from the main campus as you are."

Right now Wallace wished anything to be back in his own little world. "Excuse me, President Murray, I'm a little confused about why you sent Clarabelle for me. Have I done something, sir?"

"Have you done something?" President Murray repeated. "Yes, Mr. Bane, you have indeed done more than just one something, and that's what I need to discuss with you."

At that, Hannibal Murray walked across his office to a wall adjoining the next room and rapped on the door. Clarabelle opened it, and Wallace saw a large formal dining room beyond. "Will you please join us, Wallace?" President Murray asked him, and the president gave Clarabelle a quick wink.

As soon as Wallace entered the room he understood why the parking lot was so full. He looked around and saw most of his colleagues in the astronomy department and several other members of faculty. And then he saw Clay Arnold and Maggie Bodine, Wade and Kayla Henry, Trent Reynolds and Rebecca Willett, Sheriff Hatfield, several trustees on the college's board, and finally Laura with her parents. Wallace was stunned.

President Murray appeared at a lectern bearing Kissinger's official seal and said, "Okay, everyone, if I may please have your attention. Please find a seat everyone. We are here for a most pleasant occasion."

Wallace began to walk away to take a seat at a table in the rear when President Murray said, "Uh, Wallace, would you please remain here with me?" Wallace froze.

Hannibal Murray began, "There are a great many things that I do as president of Kissinger College, some are more pleasant than others I can assure you, but none makes me feel more fulfilled as when I can give special recognition for extraordinary effort by a member of our faculty."

President Murray nodded to Clarabelle, and she stepped forward and handed him a folder of documents.

"Wallace, far too often in our daily lives we get so wrapped up by the minutia and our own petty needs that we overlook folks who are doing exceptional work on many different levels. I have asked everyone present today to help me correct that unfortunate oversight."

It finally dawned on Wallace that he was being recognized in a very special way. He didn't know quite how to react, and he looked over at Clarabelle for guidance. She was beaming at him and giving him an enthusiastic thumbs-up. Wallace forgot himself and actually smiled broadly.

President Murray looked at the papers Clarabelle had given him and said, "I have a special resolution approved unanimously by our board of trustees that I would like to read:

- Whereas Wallace Bane has been a valued member of Kissinger College's staff for over twenty-five years, and

- Whereas Wallace Bane has been a devoted custodian of the Von Timm Observatory for a similar length of time, and

- Whereas Wallace Bane has been an internationally recognized photographer of the night sky, and as such, has brought acclaim to our college, and

- Whereas Wallace Bane has been a respectful citizen of Greencastle and Putnam County, Indiana, and

- Whereas Wallace Bane has been instrumental in assisting law enforcement agencies in solving a capital crime,

- Therefore be it resolved, that in recognition of such devotion and service to our beloved Kissinger College and the community in which we reside, that I, Hannibal Murray, president of said college, do hereby confer the honorary degree of Doctor of Arts and Sciences upon our friend and colleague, Wallace Bane."

Wallace stood next to President Murray by the lectern with a look of proud bewilderment on his face. Clarabelle Meemo stepped forward and handed a leather bound box to her uncle, the president. He stepped behind Wallace and placed a golden medallion with a purple ribbon over Wallace's head and let it rest on his chest.

"From henceforth," Hannibal Murray stated, "let it be known that Wallace Bane shall forever be recognized within our hallowed halls and across the land as Doctor Wallace Bane."

A hearty round of applause came from the audience, and Wallace broke into tears for receiving accolades that he never dreamed possible. President Murray shook his hand, and they were immediately joined by Clarabelle and all of the work friends that Wallace never knew he had. It was a very special day, indeed.

President Murray asked Wallace if he wished to say a few words. At first he was very reluctant and then he looked at Clarabelle who gestured encouragement for him to speak.

"I'm not sure what to say," he began. "This is all such a surprise, and I feel humbled beyond words. First, I wish to thank our fine president and Kissinger's board of trustees for this wonderful recognition. I'm not sure that I have done anymore than many other members of the faculty and staff on our campus, but one thing's for certain, I'm not giving it back!" he quipped. That brought thunderous laughter and another round of applause.

"Seriously, though," he began again. "I am deeply honored by your thoughtfulness. I cannot begin to adequately express my appreciation, and to have Clay Arnold and Wade Henry present today makes me even prouder. I thank you both very much. I also wish to express my sincere apologies to Ms. Bodine and Laura, and everyone really, for my petty behavior. Dr. Arnold is a photographer beyond compare, and his recognition is richly deserved."

Wallace paused to reflect for a moment. "Despite President Murray's very kind words, I have not recently behaved as honorably as I should have, and for this I can only beg your forgiveness."

Maggie stepped forward and gave Wallace a warm hug which was greeted by more applause. "All's well with us, Wallace," she said.

"And finally," Wallace began again, "I wish to thank my dear friend, Clarabelle Meemo, for helping give me the strength to do the right thing for our college, our community, and myself. She has been a friend to me like none before." He shed a tear and offered her a smile. Clarabelle took his hand.

During the hour that followed Dr. Wallace Bane was congratulated and embraced by folks who he didn't think knew his name other than "The Mole". "No more!" he thought. "I have finally taken my place among our stars."

The drive back to the brewery complex with Maggie, Tom, Rita, and Laura was briefly diverted to the Indianapolis International Airport. Laura and her parents were set to fly back home.

"Well!" Tom said with a lilt of levity in his voice. "Who said Indiana is boring?!"

Laura hugged her Aunt Maggie and me at the same time. "Please say goodbye for me again to Rennie, Mace, Tori, Weed, and Lex and Satchmo, too. You're all family to me, and you've shown me how loving families stick together."

"You're always welcome with us," I said. "We all hope you'll come back often."

Maggie and I left the airport, and I steered my Tacoma onto I-465 for the final leg of our drive home. She slid over to be next to me and laid her head on my shoulder. We both knew that the our lives would never be quite the same again with everything that had occurred. Dr. Mortimer Chestnut would be spending a long time in prison. I had my honorary doctorate. Wallace Bane finally got his just recognition, plus Clarabelle as a very special friend. Laura was safe. Maggie hadn't been abducted, and she was willing to give a retired avenging vigilante a chance. Oh, and I didn't have to execute anyone. Life is good!

I kissed the top of Maggie's auburn hair and asked if she wanted to say anything further about merging her life with mine.

She smiled at me in the rearview mirror, and simply said, "Yeah, let's go home, Doctor Dad, and see if you're as good at selecting baby names as you are wowing the world!"

~ The End ~

About the Author
Stuart Fabe

OVER THE LAST FOUR DECADES, Stuart Fabe has directed his creative energies to three artistic media: photography, weaving, and writing.

He has published several books showcasing his fine-art photography and his intricate weavings. He has exhibited artwork at numerous art shows and galleries throughout the Midwest, and his work is widely collected.

After Evening is Stuart's third novel. It is a sequel to his popular second novel, *Evening Comes*. He enjoys the role of storyteller and in examining the human conflicts inherent to vigilantism and good-versus-evil. His writing is intended solely as entertainment.

Stuart lives in the countryside near Greencastle, Indiana, with his partner, Marla Helton, two dogs, one cat, and eleven chickens.

www.ingramcontent.com/pod-product-compliance
Lightning Source LLC
Chambersburg PA
CBHW071517110726
47908CB00003B/870